Master Humphrey's Clock

Master Humphrey's Clock

by

Charles Dickens

CAMBRIDGE SCHOLARS PUBLISHING
classic texts

Master Humphrey's Clock, by Charles Dickens

This book in its current typographical format first published 2008 by

Cambridge Scholars Publishing

12 Back Chapman Street, Newcastle upon Tyne, NE6 2XX, UK

British Library Cataloguing in Publication Data
A catalogue record for this book is available from the British Library

ISBN (10): 1-84718-888-5, ISBN (13): 9781847188885

CONTENTS

CHAPTER I

MASTER HUMPHREY, FROM HIS CLOCK-SIDE IN THE CHIMNEY CORNER

THE reader must not expect to know where I live. At present, it is true, my abode may be a question of little or no import to anybody; but if I should carry my readers with me, as I hope to do, and there should spring up between them and me feelings of homely affection and regard attaching something of interest to matters ever so slightly connected with my fortunes or my speculations, even my place of residence might one day have a kind of charm for them. Bearing this possible contingency in mind, I wish them to understand, in the outset, that they must never expect to know it.

I am not a churlish old man. Friendless I can never be, for all mankind are my kindred, and I am on ill terms with no one member of my great family. But for many years I have led a lonely, solitary life;—what wound I sought to heal, what sorrow to forget, originally, matters not now; it is sufficient that retirement has become a habit with me, and that I am unwilling to break the spell which for so long a time has shed its quiet influence upon my home and heart.

I live in a venerable suburb of London, in an old house which in bygone days was a famous resort for merry roysterers and peerless ladies, long since departed. It is a silent, shady place, with a paved courtyard so full of echoes, that sometimes I am tempted to believe that faint responses to the noises of old times linger there yet, and that these ghosts of sound haunt my footsteps as I pace it up and down. I am the more confirmed in this belief, because, of late years, the echoes that attend my walks have been less loud and marked than they were wont to be; and it is pleasanter to imagine in them the rustling of silk brocade, and the light step of some lovely girl, than to recognise in their altered note the failing tread of an old man.

Those who like to read of brilliant rooms and gorgeous furniture would derive but little pleasure from a minute description of my simple dwelling. It is dear to me for the same reason that they would hold it in slight regard. Its worm-eaten doors, and low ceilings crossed by clumsy beams; its walls of wainscot, dark stairs, and gaping closets; its small chambers, communicating with each other by winding passages or narrow steps; its many nooks, scarce larger than its corner-cupboards; its very dust and dulness, are all dear to me. The moth and spider are my constant tenants; for in my house the one basks in his long sleep, and the other plies his busy loom secure and undisturbed. I have a pleasure in thinking on a summer's day how many butterflies have sprung for the first time into light and sunshine from some dark corner of these old walls.

When I first came to live here, which was many years ago, the neighbours were curious to know who I was, and whence I came, and why I lived so much alone. As time went on, and they still remained unsatisfied on these points, I became the centre of a popular ferment, extending for half a mile round, and in one direction for a full mile. Various rumours were circulated to my prejudice. I was a spy, an infidel, a conjurer, a kidnapper of children, a refugee, a priest, a monster. Mothers caught up their infants and ran into their houses as I passed; men eyed me spitefully, and muttered threats and curses. I was the object of suspicion and distrust—ay, of downright hatred too.

But when in course of time they found I did no harm, but, on the contrary, inclined towards them despite their unjust usage, they began to relent. I found my footsteps no longer dogged, as they had often been before, and observed that the women and children no longer retreated, but would stand and gaze at me as I passed their doors. I took this for a good omen, and waited patiently for better times. By degrees I began to make friends among these humble folks; and though they were yet shy of speaking, would give them 'good day,' and so pass on. In a little time, those whom I had thus accosted would make a point of coming to their doors and windows at the usual hour, and nod or courtesy to me; children, too, came timidly within my reach, and ran away quite scared when I patted their heads and bade them be good at school. These little people soon grew more familiar. From exchanging mere words of course with my older neighbours, I gradually became their friend and adviser, the depositary of their cares and sorrows, and sometimes, it may be, the reliever, in my small way, of their distresses. And now I never walk abroad but pleasant recognitions and smiling faces wait on Master Humphrey.

It was a whim of mine, perhaps as a whet to the curiosity of my neighbours, and a kind of retaliation upon them for their suspicions—it was, I say, a whim of mine, when I first took up my abode in this place, to acknowledge no other name than Humphrey. With my detractors, I was Ugly Humphrey. When I began to convert them into friends, I was Mr. Humphrey and Old Mr. Humphrey. At length I settled down into plain Master Humphrey, which was understood to be the title most pleasant to my ear; and so completely a matter of course has it become, that sometimes when I am taking my morning walk in my little courtyard, I overhear my barber—who has a profound respect for me, and would not, I am sure, abridge my honours for the world—holding forth on the other side of the wall, touching the state of 'Master Humphrey's' health, and communicating to some friend the substance of the conversation that he and Master Humphrey have had together in the course of the shaving which he has just concluded.

That I may not make acquaintance with my readers under false pretences, or give them cause to complain hereafter that I have withheld any matter which it was essential for them to have learnt at first, I wish them to know—and I smile sorrowfully to think that the time has been when the confession would have given me pain—that I am a misshapen, deformed old man.

I have never been made a misanthrope by this cause. I have never been stung by any insult, nor wounded by any jest upon my crooked figure. As a child I was melancholy and timid, but that was because the gentle consideration paid to my misfortune sunk deep into my spirit and made me sad, even in those early days. I was but a very young creature when my poor mother died, and yet I remember that often when I hung around her neck, and oftener still when I played about the room before her, she would catch me to her bosom, and bursting into tears, would soothe me with every term of fondness and affection. God knows I was a happy child at those times,—happy to nestle in her breast,—happy to weep when she did,—happy in not knowing why.

These occasions are so strongly impressed upon my memory, that they seem to have occupied whole years. I had numbered very, very few when they ceased for ever, but before then their meaning had been revealed to me.

I do not know whether all children are imbued with a quick perception of childish grace and beauty, and a strong love for it, but I was. I had no thought that I remember, either that I possessed it myself or that I lacked it, but I admired it with an intensity that I cannot describe. A little knot of playmates—they must have been beautiful, for I see them now—were clustered one day round my mother's knee in eager admiration of some picture representing a group of infant angels, which she held in her hand. Whose the picture was, whether it was familiar to me or otherwise, or how all the children came to be there, I forget; I have some dim thought it was my birthday, but the beginning of my recollection is that we were all together in a garden, and it was summer weather,—I am sure of that, for one of the little girls had roses in her sash. There were many lovely angels in this picture, and I remember the fancy coming upon me to point out which of them represented each child there, and that when I had gone through my companions, I stopped and hesitated, wondering which was most like me. I remember the children looking at each other, and my turning red and hot, and their crowding round to kiss me, saying that they loved me all the same; and then, and when the old sorrow came into my dear mother's mild and tender look, the truth broke upon me for the first time, and I knew, while watching my awkward and ungainly sports, how keenly she had felt for her poor crippled boy.

I used frequently to dream of it afterwards, and now my heart aches for that child as if I had never been he, when I think how often he awoke from some fairy change to his own old form, and sobbed himself to sleep again.

Well, well,—all these sorrows are past. My glancing at them may not be without its use, for it may help in some measure to explain why I have all my life been attached to the inanimate objects that people my chamber, and how I have come to look upon them rather in the light of old and constant friends, than as mere chairs and tables which a little money could replace at will.

Chief and first among all these is my Clock,—my old, cheerful, companionable Clock. How can I ever convey to others an idea of the comfort and consolation that this old Clock has been for years to me!

It is associated with my earliest recollections. It stood upon the staircase at home (I call it home still mechanically), nigh sixty years ago. I like it for that; but it is not on that account, nor because it is a quaint old thing in a huge oaken case curiously and richly carved, that I prize it as I do. I incline to it as if it were alive, and could understand and give me back the love I bear it.

And what other thing that has not life could cheer me as it does? what other thing that has not life (I will not say how few things that have) could have proved the same patient, true, untiring friend? How often have I sat in the long winter evenings feeling such society in its cricket-voice, that raising my eyes from my book and looking gratefully towards it, the face reddened by the glow of the shining fire has seemed to relax from its staid expression and to regard me kindly! how often in the summer twilight, when my thoughts have wandered back to a melancholy past, have its regular whisperings recalled them to the calm and peaceful present! how often in the dead tranquillity of night has its bell broken the oppressive silence, and seemed to give me assurance that the old clock was still a faithful watcher at my chamber-door! My easy-chair, my desk, my ancient furniture, my very books, I can scarcely bring myself to love even these last like my old clock.

It stands in a snug corner, midway between the fireside and a low arched door leading to my bedroom. Its fame is diffused so extensively throughout the neighbourhood, that I have often the satisfaction of hearing the publican, or the baker, and sometimes even the parish-clerk, petitioning my housekeeper (of whom I shall have much to say by-and-by) to inform him the exact time by Master Humphrey's clock. My barber, to whom I have referred, would sooner believe it than the sun. Nor are these its only distinctions. It has acquired, I am happy to say, another, inseparably connecting it not only with my enjoyments and reflections, but with those of other men; as I shall now relate.

I lived alone here for a long time without any friend or acquaintance. In the course of my wanderings by night and day, at all hours and seasons, in city streets and quiet country parts, I came to be familiar with certain faces, and to take it to heart as quite a heavy disappointment if they failed to present themselves each at its accustomed spot. But these were the only friends I knew, and beyond them I had none.

It happened, however, when I had gone on thus for a long time, that I formed an acquaintance with a deaf gentleman, which ripened into intimacy and close companionship. To this hour, I am ignorant of his name. It is his humour to conceal it, or he has a reason and purpose for so doing. In either case, I feel that he has a right to require a return of the trust he has reposed; and as he has never sought to discover my secret, I have never sought to penetrate his. There may have been something in this tacit confidence in each other flattering and pleasant to us both, and it may have imparted in the beginning an additional zest, perhaps, to our friendship. Be this as it may, we have grown to be like brothers, and still I only know him as the deaf gentleman.

I have said that retirement has become a habit with me. When I add, that the deaf gentleman and I have two friends, I communicate nothing which is inconsistent with that declaration. I spend many hours of every day in solitude and study, have no friends or change of friends but these, only see them at stated periods, and am supposed to be of a retired spirit by the very nature and object of our association.

We are men of secluded habits, with something of a cloud upon our early fortunes, whose enthusiasm, nevertheless, has not cooled with age, whose spirit of romance is not yet quenched, who are content to ramble through the world in a pleasant dream, rather than ever waken again to its harsh realities. We are alchemists who would extract the essence of perpetual youth from dust and ashes, tempt coy Truth in many light and airy forms from the bottom of her well, and discover one crumb of comfort or one grain of good in the commonest and least-regarded matter that passes through our crucible. Spirits of past times, creatures of imagination, and people of to-day are alike the objects of our seeking, and, unlike the objects of search with most philosophers, we can insure their coming at our command.

The deaf gentleman and I first began to beguile our days with these fancies, and our nights in communicating them to each other. We are now four. But in my room there are six old chairs, and we have decided that the two empty seats shall always be placed at our table when we meet, to remind us that we may yet increase our company by that number, if we should find two men to our mind. When one among us dies, his chair will always be set in its usual place, but never occupied again; and I have caused my will to be so drawn out, that when we are all dead the house shall be shut up, and the vacant chairs still left in their accustomed places. It is pleasant to think that even then our shades may, perhaps, assemble together as of yore we did, and join in ghostly converse.

One night in every week, as the clock strikes ten, we meet. At the second stroke of two, I am alone.

And now shall I tell how that my old servant, besides giving us note of time, and ticking cheerful encouragement of our proceedings, lends its name to our society, which for its punctuality and my love is christened 'Master Humphrey's Clock'? Now shall I tell how that in the bottom of the old dark closet, where the steady pendulum throbs and beats with healthy action, though the pulse of him who made it stood still long ago, and never moved again, there are piles of dusty papers constantly placed there by our hands, that we may link our enjoyments with my old friend, and draw means to beguile time from the heart of time itself? Shall I, or can I, tell with what a secret pride I open this repository when we meet at night, and still find new store of pleasure in my dear old Clock?

Friend and companion of my solitude! mine is not a selfish love; I would not keep your merits to myself, but disperse something of pleasant association with your image through the whole wide world; I would have men couple with your name cheerful and healthy thoughts; I would have them believe that you keep true and honest time; and how it would gladden me to know that they recognised some hearty English work in Master Humphrey's clock!

THE CLOCK-CASE

It is my intention constantly to address my readers from the chimney-corner, and I would fain hope that such accounts as I shall give them of our histories and proceedings, our quiet speculations or more busy adventures, will never be unwelcome. Lest, however, I should grow prolix in the outset by lingering too long upon our little association, confounding the enthusiasm with which I regard this chief happiness of my life with that minor degree of interest which those to whom I address myself may be supposed to feel for it, I have deemed it expedient to break off as they have seen.

But, still clinging to my old friend, and naturally desirous that all its merits should be known, I am tempted to open (somewhat irregularly and against our laws, I must admit) the clock-case. The first roll of paper on which I lay my hand is in the writing of the deaf gentleman. I shall have to speak of him in my next paper; and how can I better approach that welcome task than by prefacing it with a production of his own pen, consigned to the safe keeping of my honest Clock by his own hand?

The manuscript runs thus

INTRODUCTION TO THE GIANT CHRONICLES

Once upon a time, that is to say, in this our time,—the exact year, month, and day are of no matter,—there dwelt in the city of London a substantial citizen, who united in his single person the dignities of wholesale fruiterer, alderman, common-councilman, and member of the worshipful Company of Patten-makers; who had superadded to these extraordinary distinctions the important post and title of Sheriff, and who at length, and to crown all, stood next in rotation for the high and honourable office of Lord Mayor.

He was a very substantial citizen indeed. His face was like the full moon in a fog, with two little holes punched out for his eyes, a very ripe pear stuck on for his nose, and a wide gash to serve for a mouth. The girth of his waistcoat was hung up and lettered in his tailor's shop as an extraordinary curiosity. He breathed like a heavy snorer, and his voice in speaking came thickly forth, as if it were oppressed and stifled by feather-beds. He trod the ground like an elephant, and eat and drank like—like nothing but an alderman, as he was.

This worthy citizen had risen to his great eminence from small beginnings. He had once been a very lean, weazen little boy, never dreaming of carrying such a weight of flesh upon his bones or of money in his pockets, and glad enough to take his dinner at a baker's door, and his tea at a pump. But he had long ago forgotten all this, as it was proper that a wholesale fruiterer, alderman, common-councilman, member of the worshipful Company of Patten- makers, past sheriff, and, above all, a Lord Mayor that was to be, should; and he never forgot it more completely in all his life than on the eighth of November in the year of his election to the great golden civic chair, which was the day before his grand dinner at Guildhall.

It happened that as he sat that evening all alone in his counting- house, looking over the bill of fare for next day, and checking off the fat capons in fifties, and the turtle-soup by the hundred quarts, for his private amusement,—it happened that as he sat alone occupied in these pleasant calculations, a strange man came in and asked him how he did, adding, 'If I am half as much changed as you, sir, you have no recollection of me, I am sure.'

The strange man was not over and above well dressed, and was very far from being fat or rich-looking in any sense of the word, yet he spoke with a kind of modest confidence, and assumed an easy, gentlemanly sort of an air, to which nobody but a rich man can lawfully presume. Besides this, he interrupted the good citizen just as he had reckoned three hundred and seventy-two fat capons, and was carrying them over to the next column; and as if that were not aggravation enough, the learned recorder for the city of London had only ten minutes previously gone out at that very same door, and had turned round and said, 'Good night, my lord.' Yes, he had said, 'my lord;'—he, a man of birth and education, of the Honourable Society of the Middle Temple, Barrister-at-Law,—he who had an uncle in the House of Commons, and an aunt almost but not quite in the House of Lords (for she had married a feeble peer, and made him vote as she liked),—he, this man, this learned recorder, had said, 'my lord.' 'I'll not wait till to-morrow to give you your title, my Lord Mayor,' says he, with a bow and a smile; 'you are Lord Mayor *de facto*, if not *de jure*. Good night, my lord.'

The Lord Mayor elect thought of this, and turning to the stranger, and sternly bidding him 'go out of his private counting-house,' brought forward the three hundred and seventy-two fat capons, and went on with his account.

'Do you remember,' said the other, stepping forward,—'*Do* you remember little Joe Toddyhigh?'

The port wine fled for a moment from the fruiterer's nose as he muttered, 'Joe Toddyhigh! What about Joe Toddyhigh?'

'I am Joe Toddyhigh,' cried the visitor. 'Look at me, look hard at me,—harder, harder. You know me now? You know little Joe again? What a happiness to us both, to meet the very night before your grandeur! O! give me your hand, Jack,—both hands,—both, for the sake of old times.'

'You pinch me, sir. You're a-hurting of me,' said the Lord Mayor elect pettishly. 'Don't,—suppose anybody should come,—Mr. Toddyhigh, sir.'

'Mr. Toddyhigh!' repeated the other ruefully.

'O, don't bother,' said the Lord Mayor elect, scratching his head. 'Dear me! Why, I thought you was dead. What a fellow you are!'

Indeed, it was a pretty state of things, and worthy the tone of vexation and disappointment in which the Lord Mayor spoke. Joe Toddyhigh had been a poor boy with him at Hull, and had oftentimes divided his last penny and parted his last crust to relieve his wants; for though Joe was a destitute child in those times, he was as faithful and affectionate in his friendship as ever man of might could be. They parted one day to seek their fortunes in different directions. Joe went to sea, and the now wealthy citizen begged his way to London, They separated with many tears, like foolish fellows as they were, and agreed to remain fast friends, and if they lived, soon to communicate again.

When he was an errand-boy, and even in the early days of his apprenticeship, the citizen had many a time trudged to the Post-office to ask if there were any letter from poor little Joe, and had gone home again with tears in his eyes, when he found no news of his only friend. The world is a wide place, and it was a long time before the letter came; when it did, the writer was forgotten. It turned from white to yellow from lying in the Post-office with nobody to claim it, and in course of time was torn up with five hundred others, and sold for waste-paper. And now at last, and when it might least have been expected, here was this Joe Toddyhigh turning up and claiming acquaintance with a great public character, who on the morrow would be cracking jokes with the Prime Minister of England, and who had only, at any time during the next twelve months, to say the word, and he could shut up Temple Bar, and make it no thoroughfare for the king himself!

'I am sure I don't know what to say, Mr. Toddyhigh,' said the Lord Mayor elect; 'I really don't. It's very inconvenient. I'd sooner have given twenty pound,—it's very inconvenient, really.'—A thought had come into his mind, that perhaps his old friend might say something passionate which would give him an excuse for being angry himself. No such thing. Joe looked at him steadily, but very mildly, and did not open his lips.

'Of course I shall pay you what I owe you,' said the Lord Mayor elect, fidgeting in his chair. 'You lent me—I think it was a shilling or some small coin—when we parted company, and that of course I shall pay with good interest. I can pay my way with any man, and always have done. If you look into the Mansion House the day after to-morrow,—some time after dusk,—and ask for my private clerk, you'll find he has a draft for you. I haven't got time to say anything more just now, unless,'—he hesitated, for, coupled with a strong desire to glitter for once in all his glory in the eyes of his former companion, was a distrust of his appearance, which might be more shabby than he could tell by that feeble light,—'unless you'd like to come to the dinner to-morrow. I don't mind your having this ticket, if you like to take it. A great many people would give their ears for it, I can tell you.'

His old friend took the card without speaking a word, and instantly departed. His sunburnt face and gray hair were present to the citizen's mind for a moment; but by the time he reached three hundred and eighty-one fat capons, he had quite forgotten him.

Joe Toddyhigh had never been in the capital of Europe before, and he wandered up and down the streets that night amazed at the number of churches and other public buildings, the splendour of the shops, the riches that were heaped up on every side, the glare of light in which they were displayed, and the concourse of people who hurried to and fro, indifferent, apparently, to all the wonders that surrounded them. But in all the long streets and broad squares, there were none but strangers; it was quite a relief to turn down a by-way and hear his own footsteps on the pavement. He went home to his inn, thought that London was a dreary, desolate place, and felt disposed to doubt the existence of one true-hearted man in the whole worshipful Company of Patten-makers. Finally, he went to bed, and dreamed that he and the Lord Mayor elect were boys again.

He went next day to the dinner; and when in a burst of light and music, and in the midst of splendid decorations and surrounded by brilliant company, his former friend appeared at the head of the Hall, and was hailed with shouts and cheering, he cheered and shouted with the best, and for the moment could have cried. The next moment he cursed his weakness in behalf of a man so changed and selfish, and quite hated a jolly-looking old gentleman opposite for declaring himself in the pride of his heart a Patten-maker.

As the banquet proceeded, he took more and more to heart the rich citizen's unkindness; and that, not from any envy, but because he felt that a man of his state and fortune could all the better afford to recognise an old friend, even if he were poor and obscure. The more he thought of this, the more lonely and sad he felt. When the company dispersed and adjourned to the ball-room, he paced the hall and passages alone, ruminating in a very melancholy condition upon the disappointment he had experienced.

It chanced, while he was lounging about in this moody state, that he stumbled upon a flight of stairs, dark, steep, and narrow, which he ascended without any thought about the matter, and so came into a little music-gallery, empty and deserted. From this elevated post, which commanded the whole hall, he amused himself in looking down upon the attendants who were clearing away the fragments of the feast very lazily, and drinking out of all the bottles and glasses with most commendable perseverance.

His attention gradually relaxed, and he fell fast asleep.

When he awoke, he thought there must be something the matter with his eyes; but, rubbing them a little, he soon found that the moonlight was really streaming through the east window, that the lamps were all extinguished, and that he was alone. He listened, but no distant murmur in the echoing passages, not even the shutting of a door, broke the deep silence; he groped his way down the stairs, and found that the door at the bottom was locked on the other side. He began now to comprehend that he must have slept a long time, that he had been overlooked, and was shut up there for the night.

His first sensation, perhaps, was not altogether a comfortable one, for it was a dark, chilly, earthy-smelling place, and something too large, for a man so situated, to feel at home in. However, when the momentary consternation of his surprise was over, he made light of the accident, and resolved to feel his way up the stairs again, and make himself as comfortable as he could in the gallery until morning. As he turned to execute this purpose, he heard the clocks strike three.

Any such invasion of a dead stillness as the striking of distant clocks, causes it to appear the more intense and insupportable when the sound has ceased. He listened with strained attention in the hope that some clock, lagging behind its fellows, had yet to strike,—looking all the time into the profound darkness before him, until it seemed to weave itself into a black tissue, patterned with a hundred reflections of his own eyes. But the bells had all pealed out their warning for that once, and the gust of wind that moaned through the place seemed cold and heavy with their iron breath.

The time and circumstances were favourable to reflection. He tried to keep his thoughts to the current, unpleasant though it was, in which they had moved all day, and to think with what a romantic feeling he had looked forward to shaking his old friend by the hand before he died, and what a wide and cruel difference there was between the meeting they had had, and that which he had so often and so long anticipated. Still, he was disordered by waking to such sudden loneliness, and could not prevent his mind from running upon odd tales of people of undoubted courage, who, being shut up by night in vaults or churches, or other dismal places, had scaled great heights to get out, and fled from silence as they had never done from danger. This brought to his mind the moonlight through the window, and bethinking himself of it, he groped his way back up the crooked stairs,—but very stealthily, as though he were fearful of being overheard.

He was very much astonished when he approached the gallery again, to see a light in the building: still more so, on advancing hastily and looking round, to observe no visible source from which it could proceed. But how much greater yet was his astonishment at the spectacle which this light revealed.

The statues of the two giants, Gog and Magog, each above fourteen feet in height, those which succeeded to still older and more barbarous figures, after the Great Fire of London, and which stand in the Guildhall to this day, were endowed with life and motion. These guardian genii of the City had quitted their pedestals, and reclined in easy attitudes in the great stained glass window. Between them was an ancient cask, which seemed to be full of wine; for the younger Giant, clapping his huge hand upon it, and throwing up his mighty leg, burst into an exulting laugh, which reverberated through the hall like thunder.

Joe Toddyhigh instinctively stooped down, and, more dead than alive, felt his hair stand on end, his knees knock together, and a cold damp break out upon his forehead. But even at that minute curiosity prevailed over every other feeling, and somewhat reassured by the good-humour of the Giants and their apparent unconsciousness of his presence, he crouched in a corner of the gallery, in as small a space as he could, and, peeping between the rails, observed them closely.

It was then that the elder Giant, who had a flowing gray beard, raised his thoughtful eyes to his companion's face, and in a grave and solemn voice addressed him thus:

FIRST NIGHT OF THE GIANT CHRONICLES

Turning towards his companion the elder Giant uttered these words in a grave, majestic tone:

'Magog, does boisterous mirth beseem the Giant Warder of this ancient city? Is this becoming demeanour for a watchful spirit over whose bodiless head so many years have rolled, so many changes swept like empty air—in whose impalpable nostrils the scent of blood and crime, pestilence, cruelty, and horror, has been familiar as breath to mortals—in whose sight Time has gathered in the harvest of centuries, and garnered so many crops of human pride, affections, hopes, and sorrows? Bethink you of our compact. The night wanes; feasting, revelry, and music have encroached upon our usual hours of solitude, and morning will be here apace. Ere we are stricken mute again, bethink you of our compact.'

Pronouncing these latter words with more of impatience than quite accorded with his apparent age and gravity, the Giant raised a long pole (which he still bears in his hand) and tapped his brother Giant rather smartly on the head; indeed, the blow was so smartly administered, that the latter quickly withdrew his lips from the cask, to which they had been applied, and, catching up his shield and halberd, assumed an attitude of defence. His irritation was but momentary, for he laid these weapons aside as hastily as he had assumed them, and said as he did so:

'You know, Gog, old friend, that when we animate these shapes which the Londoners of old assigned (and not unworthily) to the guardian genii of their city, we are susceptible of some of the sensations which belong to human kind. Thus when I taste wine, I feel blows; when I relish the one, I disrelish the other. Therefore, Gog, the more especially as your arm is none of the lightest, keep your good staff by your side, else we may chance to differ. Peace be between us!'

'Amen!' said the other, leaning his staff in the window-corner. 'Why did you laugh just now?'

'To think,' replied the Giant Magog, laying his hand upon the cask, 'of him who owned this wine, and kept it in a cellar hoarded from the light of day, for thirty years,—"till it should be fit to drink," quoth he. He was twoscore and ten years old when he buried it beneath his house, and yet never thought that he might be scarcely "fit to drink" when the wine became so. I wonder it never occurred to him to make himself unfit to be eaten. There is very little of him left by this time.'

'The night is waning,' said Gog mournfully.

'I know it,' replied his companion, 'and I see you are impatient. But look. Through the eastern window—placed opposite to us, that the first beams of the rising sun may every morning gild our giant faces—the moon-rays fall upon the pavement in a stream of light that to my fancy sinks through the cold stone and gushes into the old crypt below. The night is scarcely past its noon, and our great charge is sleeping heavily.'

They ceased to speak, and looked upward at the moon. The sight of their large, black, rolling eyes filled Joe Toddyhigh with such horror that he could scarcely draw his breath. Still they took no note of him, and appeared to believe themselves quite alone.

'Our compact,' said Magog after a pause, 'is, if I understand it, that, instead of watching here in silence through the dreary nights, we entertain each other with stories of our past experience; with tales of the past, the present, and the future; with legends of London and her sturdy citizens from the old simple times. That every night at midnight, when St. Paul's bell tolls out one, and we may move and speak, we thus discourse, nor leave such themes till the first gray gleam of day shall strike us dumb. Is that our bargain, brother?'

'Yes,' said the Giant Gog, 'that is the league between us who guard this city, by day in spirit, and by night in body also; and never on ancient holidays have its conduits run wine more merrily than we will pour forth our legendary lore. We are old chroniclers from this time hence. The crumbled walls encircle us once more, the postern-gates are closed, the drawbridge is up, and pent in its narrow den beneath, the water foams and struggles with the sunken starlings. Jerkins and quarter-staves are in the streets again, the nightly watch is set, the rebel, sad and lonely in his Tower dungeon, tries to sleep and weeps for home and children. Aloft upon the gates and walls are noble heads glaring fiercely down upon the dreaming city, and vexing the hungry dogs that scent them in the air, and tear the ground beneath with dismal howlings. The axe, the block, the rack, in their dark chambers give signs of recent use. The Thames, floating past long lines of cheerful windows whence come a burst of music and a stream of light, bears suddenly to the Palace wall the last red stain brought on the tide from Traitor's Gate. But your pardon, brother. The night wears, and I am talking idly.'

The other Giant appeared to be entirely of this opinion, for during the foregoing rhapsody of his fellow-sentinel he had been scratching his head with an air of comical uneasiness, or rather with an air that would have been very comical if he had been a dwarf or an ordinary-sized man. He winked too, and though it could not be doubted for a moment that he winked to himself, still he certainly cocked his enormous eye towards the gallery where the listener was concealed. Nor was this all, for he gaped; and when he gaped, Joe was horribly reminded of the popular prejudice on the subject of giants, and of their fabled power of smelling out Englishmen, however closely concealed.

His alarm was such that he nearly swooned, and it was some little time before his power of sight or hearing was restored. When he recovered he found that the elder Giant was pressing the younger to commence the Chronicles, and that the latter was endeavouring to excuse himself on the ground that the night was far spent, and it would be better to wait until the next. Well assured by this that he was certainly about to begin directly, the listener collected his faculties by a great effort, and distinctly heard Magog express himself to the following effect:—

In the sixteenth century and in the reign of Queen Elizabeth of glorious memory (albeit her golden days are sadly rusted with blood), there lived in the city of London a bold young 'prentice who loved his master's daughter. There were no doubt within the walls a great many 'prentices in this condition, but I speak of only one, and his name was Hugh Graham.

This Hugh was apprenticed to an honest Bowyer who dwelt in the ward of Cheype, and was rumoured to possess great wealth. Rumour was quite as infallible in those days as at the present time, but it happened then as now to be sometimes right by accident. It stumbled upon the truth when it gave the old Bowyer a mint of money. His trade had been a profitable one in the time of King Henry the Eighth, who encouraged English archery to the utmost, and he had been prudent and discreet. Thus it came to pass that Mistress Alice, his only daughter, was the richest heiress in all his wealthy ward. Young Hugh had often maintained with staff and cudgel that she was the handsomest. To do him justice, I believe she was.

If he could have gained the heart of pretty Mistress Alice by knocking this conviction into stubborn people's heads, Hugh would have had no cause to fear. But though the Bowyer's daughter smiled in secret to hear of his doughty deeds for her sake, and though her little waiting-woman reported all her smiles (and many more) to Hugh, and though he was at a vast expense in kisses and small coin to recompense her fidelity, he made no progress in his love. He durst not whisper it to

Mistress Alice save on sure encouragement, and that she never gave him. A glance of her dark eye as she sat at the door on a summer's evening after prayer-time, while he and the neighbouring 'prentices exercised themselves in the street with blunted sword and buckler, would fire Hugh's blood so that none could stand before him; but then she glanced at others quite as kindly as on him, and where was the use of cracking crowns if Mistress Alice smiled upon the cracked as well as on the cracker?

Still Hugh went on, and loved her more and more. He thought of her all day, and dreamed of her all night long. He treasured up her every word and gesture, and had a palpitation of the heart whenever he heard her footstep on the stairs or her voice in an adjoining room. To him, the old Bowyer's house was haunted by an angel; there was enchantment in the air and space in which she moved. It would have been no miracle to Hugh if flowers had sprung from the rush-strewn floors beneath the tread of lovely Mistress Alice.

Never did 'prentice long to distinguish himself in the eyes of his lady-love so ardently as Hugh. Sometimes he pictured to himself the house taking fire by night, and he, when all drew back in fear, rushing through flame and smoke, and bearing her from the ruins in his arms. At other times he thought of a rising of fierce rebels, an attack upon the city, a strong assault upon the Bowyer's house in particular, and he falling on the threshold pierced with numberless wounds in defence of Mistress Alice. If he could only enact some prodigy of valour, do some wonderful deed, and let her know that she had inspired it, he thought he could die contented.

Sometimes the Bowyer and his daughter would go out to supper with a worthy citizen at the fashionable hour of six o'clock, and on such occasions Hugh, wearing his blue 'prentice cloak as gallantly as 'prentice might, would attend with a lantern and his trusty club to escort them home. These were the brightest moments of his life. To hold the light while Mistress Alice picked her steps, to touch her hand as he helped her over broken ways, to have her leaning on his arm,—it sometimes even came to that,—this was happiness indeed!

When the nights were fair, Hugh followed in the rear, his eyes riveted on the graceful figure of the Bowyer's daughter as she and the old man moved on before him. So they threaded the narrow winding streets of the city, now passing beneath the overhanging gables of old wooden houses whence creaking signs projected into the street, and now emerging from some dark and frowning gateway into the clear moonlight. At such times, or when the shouts of straggling brawlers met her ear, the Bowyer's daughter would look timidly back at Hugh, beseeching him to draw nearer, and then how he grasped his club and longed to do battle with a dozen rufflers, for the love of Mistress Alice!

The old Bowyer was in the habit of lending money on interest to the gallants of the Court, and thus it happened that many a richly- dressed gentleman dismounted at his door. More waving plumes and gallant steeds, indeed, were seen at the Bowyer's house, and more embroidered silks and velvets sparkled in his dark shop and darker private closet, than at any merchants in the city. In those times no less than in the present it would seem that the richest-looking cavaliers often wanted money the most.

Of these glittering clients there was one who always came alone. He was nobly mounted, and, having no attendant, gave his horse in charge to Hugh while he and the Bowyer were closeted within. Once as he sprung into the saddle Mistress Alice was seated at an upper window, and before she could withdraw he had doffed his jewelled cap and kissed his hand. Hugh watched him caracoling down the street, and burnt with indignation. But how much deeper was the glow that reddened in his cheeks when, raising his eyes to the casement, he saw that Alice watched the stranger too!

He came again and often, each time arrayed more gaily than before, and still the little casement showed him Mistress Alice. At length one heavy day, she fled from home. It had cost her a hard struggle, for all her old father's gifts were strewn about her chamber as if she had parted from them one by one, and knew that the time must come when these tokens of his love would wring her heart,—yet she was gone.

She left a letter commanding her poor father to the care of Hugh, and wishing he might be happier than ever he could have been with her, for he deserved the love of a better and a purer heart than she had to bestow. The old man's forgiveness (she said) she had no power to ask, but she prayed God to bless him,—and so ended with a blot upon the paper where her tears had fallen.

At first the old man's wrath was kindled, and he carried his wrong to the Queen's throne itself; but there was no redress he learnt at Court, for his daughter had been conveyed abroad. This afterwards appeared to be the truth, as there came from France, after an interval of several years, a letter in her hand. It was written in trembling characters, and almost illegible. Little could be made out save that she often thought of home and her old dear pleasant room,—and that she had dreamt her father was dead and had not blessed her,—and that her heart was breaking.

The poor old Bowyer lingered on, never suffering Hugh to quit his sight, for he knew now that he had loved his daughter, and that was the only link that bound him to earth. It broke at length and he died,—bequeathing his old 'prentice his trade and all his wealth, and solemnly charging him with his last breath to revenge his child if ever he who had worked her misery crossed his path in life again.

From the time of Alice's flight, the tilting-ground, the fields, the fencing-school, the summer-evening sports, knew Hugh no more. His spirit was dead within him. He rose to great eminence and repute among the citizens, but was seldom seen to smile, and never mingled in their revelries or rejoicings. Brave, humane, and generous, he was beloved by all. He was pitied too by those who knew his story, and these were so many that when he walked along the streets alone at dusk, even the rude common people doffed their caps and mingled a rough air of sympathy with their respect.

One night in May—it was her birthnight, and twenty years since she had left her home—Hugh Graham sat in the room she had hallowed in his boyish days. He was now a gray-haired man, though still in the prime of life. Old thoughts had borne him company for many hours, and the chamber had gradually grown quite dark, when he was roused by a low knocking at the outer door.

He hastened down, and opening it saw by the light of a lamp which he had seized upon the way, a female figure crouching in the portal. It hurried swiftly past him and glided up the stairs. He looked for pursuers. There were none in sight. No, not one.

He was inclined to think it a vision of his own brain, when suddenly a vague suspicion of the truth flashed upon his mind. He barred the door, and hastened wildly back. Yes, there she was,—there, in the chamber he had quitted,—there in her old innocent, happy home, so changed that none but he could trace one gleam of what she had been,—there upon her knees,—with her hands clasped in agony and shame before her burning face.

'My God, my God!' she cried, 'now strike me dead! Though I have brought death and shame and sorrow on this roof, O, let me die at home in mercy!'

There was no tear upon her face then, but she trembled and glanced round the chamber. Everything was in its old place. Her bed looked as if she had risen from it but that morning. The sight of these familiar objects, marking the dear remembrance in which she had been held, and the blight she had brought upon herself, was more than the woman's better nature that had carried her there could bear. She wept and fell upon the ground.

A rumour was spread about, in a few days' time, that the Bowyer's cruel daughter had come home, and that Master Graham had given her lodging in his house. It was rumoured too that he had resigned her fortune, in order that she might bestow it in acts of charity, and that he had vowed to guard her in her solitude, but that they were never to see each other more. These rumours greatly incensed all virtuous wives and daughters in the ward, especially when they appeared to receive some corroboration from the circumstance of Master Graham taking up his abode in another tenement hard by. The estimation in which he was held, however, forbade any questioning on the subject; and as the Bowyer's house was close shut up, and nobody came forth when public shows and festivities were in progress, or to flaunt in the public walks, or to buy new fashions at the mercers' booths, all the well-conducted females agreed among themselves that there could be no woman there.

These reports had scarcely died away when the wonder of every good citizen, male and female, was utterly absorbed and swallowed up by a Royal Proclamation, in which her Majesty, strongly censuring the practice of wearing long Spanish rapiers of preposterous length (as being a bullying and swaggering custom, tending to bloodshed and public disorder), commanded that on a particular day therein named, certain grave citizens should repair to the city gates, and there, in public, break all rapiers worn or carried by persons claiming admission, that exceeded, though it were only by a quarter of an inch, three standard feet in length.

Royal Proclamations usually take their course, let the public wonder never so much. On the appointed day two citizens of high repute took up their stations at each of the gates, attended by a party of the city guard, the main body to enforce the Queen's will, and take custody of all such rebels (if any) as might have the temerity to dispute it: and a few to bear the standard measures and instruments for reducing all unlawful sword-blades to the prescribed dimensions. In pursuance of these arrangements, Master Graham and another were posted at Lud Gate, on the hill before St. Paul's.

A pretty numerous company were gathered together at this spot, for, besides the officers in attendance to enforce the proclamation, there was a motley crowd of lookers-on of various degrees, who raised from time to time such shouts and cries as the circumstances called forth. A spruce young courtier was the first who approached: he unsheathed a weapon of burnished steel that shone and glistened in the sun, and handed it with the newest air to the officer, who, finding it exactly three feet long, returned it with a bow. Thereupon the gallant raised his hat and crying, 'God save the Queen!' passed on amidst the plaudits of the mob. Then came another—a better courtier still—who wore a blade but two feet long, whereat the people laughed, much to the disparagement of his honour's dignity. Then came a third, a sturdy old officer of the army, girded with a rapier at least a foot and a half beyond her Majesty's pleasure; at him they raised a great shout, and most of the spectators (but especially those who were armourers or cutlers) laughed very heartily at the breakage which would ensue. But they were disappointed; for the old campaigner, coolly unbuckling his sword and bidding his servant carry it home again, passed through unarmed, to the great indignation of all the beholders. They relieved themselves in some degree by hooting a tall blustering fellow with a prodigious weapon, who stopped short on coming in sight of the preparations, and after a little consideration turned back again. But all this time no rapier had been broken, although it was high noon, and all cavaliers of any quality or appearance were taking their way towards Saint Paul's churchyard.

During these proceedings, Master Graham had stood apart, strictly confining himself to the duty imposed upon him, and taking little heed of anything beyond. He stepped forward now as a richly- dressed gentleman on foot, followed by a single attendant, was seen advancing up the hill.

As this person drew nearer, the crowd stopped their clamour, and bent forward with eager looks. Master Graham standing alone in the gateway, and the stranger coming slowly towards him, they seemed, as it were, set face to face. The nobleman (for he looked one) had a haughty and disdainful air, which bespoke the slight estimation in which he held the citizen. The citizen, on the other hand, preserved the resolute bearing of one who was not to be frowned down or daunted, and who cared very little for any nobility but that of worth and manhood. It was perhaps some consciousness on the part of each, of these feelings in the other, that infused a more stern expression into their regards as they came closer together.

'Your rapier, worthy sir!'

At the instant that he pronounced these words Graham started, and falling back some paces, laid his hand upon the dagger in his belt.

'You are the man whose horse I used to hold before the Bowyer's door? You are that man? Speak!'

'Out, you 'prentice hound!' said the other.

'You are he! I know you well now!' cried Graham. 'Let no man step between us two, or I shall be his murderer.' With that he drew his dagger, and rushed in upon him.

The stranger had drawn his weapon from the scabbard ready for the scrutiny, before a word was spoken. He made a thrust at his assailant, but the dagger which Graham clutched in his left hand being the dirk in use at that time for parrying such blows, promptly turned the point aside. They closed. The dagger fell rattling on the ground, and Graham, wresting his adversary's sword from his grasp, plunged it through his heart. As he drew it out it snapped in two, leaving a fragment in the dead man's body.

All this passed so swiftly that the bystanders looked on without an effort to interfere; but the man was no sooner down than an uproar broke forth which rent the air. The attendant rushing through the gate proclaimed that his master, a nobleman, had been set upon and slain by a citizen; the word quickly spread from mouth to mouth; Saint Paul's Cathedral, and every book-shop, ordinary, and smoking- house in the churchyard poured out its stream of cavaliers and their followers, who mingling together in a dense tumultuous body, struggled, sword in hand, towards the spot.

With equal impetuosity, and stimulating each other by loud cries and shouts, the citizens and common people took up the quarrel on their side, and encircling Master Graham a hundred deep, forced him from the gate. In vain he waved the broken sword above his head, crying that he would die on London's threshold for their sacred homes. They bore him on, and ever keeping him in the midst, so that no man could attack him, fought their way into the city.

The clash of swords and roar of voices, the dust and heat and pressure, the trampling under foot of men, the distracted looks and shrieks of women at the windows above as they recognised their relatives or lovers in the crowd, the rapid tolling of alarm-bells, the furious rage and passion of the scene, were fearful. Those who, being on the outskirts of each crowd, could use their weapons with effect, fought desperately, while those behind, maddened with baffled rage, struck at each other over the heads of those before them, and crushed their own fellows. Wherever the broken sword was seen above the people's heads, towards that spot the cavaliers made a new rush. Every one of these charges was marked by sudden gaps in the throng where men were trodden down, but as fast as they were made, the tide swept over them, and still the multitude pressed on again, a confused mass of swords, clubs, staves, broken plumes, fragments of rich cloaks and doublets, and angry, bleeding faces, all mixed up together in inextricable disorder.

The design of the people was to force Master Graham to take refuge in his dwelling, and to defend it until the authorities could interfere, or they could gain time for parley. But either from ignorance or in the confusion of the moment they stopped at his old house, which was closely shut. Some time was lost in beating the doors open and passing him to the front. About a score of the boldest of the other party threw themselves into the torrent while this was being done, and reaching the door at the same moment with himself cut him off from his defenders.

'I never will turn in such a righteous cause, so help me Heaven!' cried Graham, in a voice that at last made itself heard, and confronting them as he spoke. 'Least of all will I turn upon this threshold which owes its desolation to such men as ye. I give no quarter, and I will have none! Strike!'

For a moment they stood at bay. At that moment a shot from an unseen hand, apparently fired by some person who had gained access to one of the opposite houses, struck Graham in the brain, and he fell dead. A low wail was heard in the air,—many people in the concourse cried that they had seen a spirit glide across the little casement window of the Bowyer's house—

A dead silence succeeded. After a short time some of the flushed and heated throng laid down their arms and softly carried the body within doors. Others fell off or slunk away in knots of two or three, others whispered together in groups, and before a numerous guard which then rode up could muster in the street, it was nearly empty.

Those who carried Master Graham to the bed up-stairs were shocked to see a woman lying beneath the window with her hands clasped together. After trying to recover her in vain, they laid her near the citizen, who still retained, tightly grasped in his right hand, the first and last sword that was broken that day at Lud Gate.

* * * * *

The Giant uttered these concluding words with sudden precipitation; and on the instant the strange light which had filled the hall faded away. Joe Toddyhigh glanced involuntarily at the eastern window, and saw the first pale gleam of morning. He turned his head again towards the other window in which the Giants had been seated. It was empty. The cask of wine was gone, and he could dimly make out that the two great figures stood mute and motionless upon their pedestals.

After rubbing his eyes and wondering for full half an hour, during which time he observed morning come creeping on apace, he yielded to the drowsiness which overpowered him and fell into a refreshing slumber. When he awoke it was broad day; the building was open, and workmen were busily engaged in removing the vestiges of last night's feast.

Stealing gently down the little stairs, and assuming the air of some early lounger who had dropped in from the street, he walked up to the foot of each pedestal in turn, and attentively examined the figure it supported. There could be no doubt about the features of either; he recollected the exact expression they had worn at different passages of their conversation, and recognised in every line and lineament the Giants of the night. Assured that it was no vision, but that he had heard and seen with his own proper senses, he walked forth, determining at all hazards to conceal himself in the Guildhall again that evening. He further resolved to sleep all day, so that he might be very wakeful and vigilant, and above all that he might take notice of the figures at the precise moment of their becoming animated and subsiding into their old state, which he greatly reproached himself for not having done already.

CORRESPONDENCE

TO MASTER HUMPHREY

'SIR,—Before you proceed any further in your account of your friends and what you say and do when you meet together, excuse me if I proffer my claim to be elected to one of the vacant chairs in that old room of yours. Don't reject me without full consideration; for if you do, you will be sorry for it afterwards—you will, upon my life.

'I enclose my card, sir, in this letter. I never was ashamed of my name, and I never shall be. I am considered a devilish gentlemanly fellow, and I act up to the character. If you want a reference, ask any of the men at our club. Ask any fellow who goes there to write his letters, what sort of conversation mine is. Ask him if he thinks I have the sort of voice that will suit your deaf friend and make him hear, if he can hear anything at all. Ask the servants what they think of me. There's not a rascal among 'em, sir, but will tremble to hear my name. That reminds me—don't you say too much about that housekeeper of yours; it's a low subject, damned low.

'I tell you what, sir. If you vote me into one of those empty chairs, you'll have among you a man with a fund of gentlemanly information that'll rather astonish you. I can let you into a few anecdotes about some fine women of title, that are quite high life, sir—the tiptop sort of thing. I know the name of every man who has been out on an affair of honour within the last five-and-twenty years; I know the private particulars of every cross and squabble that has taken place upon the turf, at the gaming-table, or elsewhere, during the whole of that time. I have been called the gentlemanly chronicle. You may consider yourself a lucky dog; upon my soul, you may congratulate yourself, though I say so.

'It's an uncommon good notion that of yours, not letting anybody know where you live. I have tried it, but there has always been an anxiety respecting me, which has found me out. Your deaf friend is a cunning fellow to keep his name so close. I have tried that too, but have always failed. I shall be proud to make his acquaintance—tell him so, with my compliments.

'You must have been a queer fellow when you were a child, confounded queer. It's odd, all that about the picture in your first paper—prosy, but told in a devilish gentlemanly sort of way. In places like that I could come in with great effect with a touch of life—don't you feel that?

'I am anxiously waiting for your next paper to know whether your friends live upon the premises, and at your expense, which I take it for granted is the case. If I am right in this impression, I know a charming fellow (an excellent companion and most delightful company) who will be proud to join you. Some years ago he seconded a great many prize-fighters, and once fought an amateur match himself; since then he has driven several mails, broken at different periods all the lamps on the right-hand side of Oxford-street, and six times carried away every bell-handle in Bloomsbury-square, besides turning off the gas in various thoroughfares. In point of gentlemanliness he is unrivalled, and I should say that next to myself he is of all men the best suited to your purpose.

'Expecting your reply,
'I am,
'&c. &c.'

Master Humphrey informs this gentleman that his application, both as it concerns himself and his friend, is rejected.

CHAPTER II

MASTER HUMPHREY, FROM HIS CLOCK-SIDE IN THE CHIMNEY-CORNER

MY old companion tells me it is midnight. The fire glows brightly, crackling with a sharp and cheerful sound, as if it loved to burn. The merry cricket on the hearth (my constant visitor), this ruddy blaze, my clock, and I, seem to share the world among us, and to be the only things awake. The wind, high and boisterous but now, has died away and hoarsely mutters in its sleep. I love all times and seasons each in its turn, and am apt, perhaps, to think the present one the best; but past or coming I always love this peaceful time of night, when long-buried thoughts, favoured by the gloom and silence, steal from their graves, and haunt the scenes of faded happiness and hope.

The popular faith in ghosts has a remarkable affinity with the whole current of our thoughts at such an hour as this, and seems to be their necessary and natural consequence. For who can wonder that man should feel a vague belief in tales of disembodied spirits wandering through those places which they once dearly affected, when he himself, scarcely less separated from his old world than they, is for ever lingering upon past emotions and bygone times, and hovering, the ghost of his former self, about the places and people that warmed his heart of old? It is thus that at this quiet hour I haunt the house where I was born, the rooms I used to tread, the scenes of my infancy, my boyhood, and my youth; it is thus that I prowl around my buried treasure (though not of gold or silver), and mourn my loss; it is thus that I revisit the ashes of extinguished fires, and take my silent stand at old bedsides. If my spirit should ever glide back to this chamber when my body is mingled with the dust, it will but follow the course it often took in the old man's lifetime, and add but one more change to the subjects of its contemplation.

In all my idle speculations I am greatly assisted by various legends connected with my venerable house, which are current in the neighbourhood, and are so numerous that there is scarce a cupboard or corner that has not some dismal story of its own. When I first entertained thoughts of becoming its tenant, I was assured that it was haunted from roof to cellar, and I believe that the bad opinion in which my neighbours once held me, had its rise in my not being torn to pieces, or at least distracted with terror, on the night I took possession; in either of which cases I should doubtless have arrived by a short cut at the very summit of popularity.

But traditions and rumours all taken into account, who so abets me in every fancy and chimes with my every thought, as my dear deaf friend? and how often have I cause to bless the day that brought us two together! Of all days in the year I rejoice to think that it should have been Christmas Day, with which from childhood we associate something friendly, hearty, and sincere.

I had walked out to cheer myself with the happiness of others, and, in the little tokens of festivity and rejoicing, of which the streets and houses present so many upon that day, had lost some hours. Now I stopped to look at a merry party hurrying through the snow on foot to their place of meeting, and now turned back to see a whole coachful of children safely deposited at the welcome house. At one time, I admired how carefully the working man carried the baby in its gaudy hat and feathers, and how his wife, trudging patiently on behind, forgot even her care of her gay clothes, in exchanging greeting with the child as it crowed and laughed over the father's shoulder; at another, I pleased myself with some passing scene of gallantry or courtship, and was glad to believe that for a season half the world of poverty was gay.

As the day closed in, I still rambled through the streets, feeling a companionship in the bright fires that cast their warm reflection on the windows as I passed, and losing all sense of my own loneliness in imagining the sociality and kind-fellowship that everywhere prevailed. At length I happened to stop before a Tavern, and, encountering a Bill of Fare in the window, it all at once brought it into my head to wonder what kind of people dined alone in Taverns upon Christmas Day.

Solitary men are accustomed, I suppose, unconsciously to look upon solitude as their own peculiar property. I had sat alone in my room on many, many anniversaries of this great holiday, and had never regarded it but as one of universal assemblage and rejoicing. I had excepted, and with an aching heart, a crowd of prisoners and beggars; but *these* were not the men for whom the Tavern doors were open. Had they any customers, or was it a mere form?—a form, no doubt.

Trying to feel quite sure of this, I walked away; but before I had gone many paces, I stopped and looked back. There was a provoking air of business in the lamp above the door which I could not overcome. I began to be afraid there might be many customers—young men, perhaps, struggling with the world, utter strangers in this great place, whose friends lived at a long distance off, and whose means were too slender to enable them to make the journey. The supposition gave rise to so many distressing little pictures, that in preference to carrying them home with me, I determined to encounter the realities. So I turned and walked in.

I was at once glad and sorry to find that there was only one person in the dining-room; glad to know that there were not more, and sorry that he should be there by himself. He did not look so old as I, but like me he was advanced in life, and his hair was nearly white. Though I made more noise in entering and seating myself than was quite necessary, with the view of attracting his attention and saluting him in the good old form of that time of year, he did not raise his head, but sat with it resting on his hand, musing over his half-finished meal.

I called for something which would give me an excuse for remaining in the room (I had dined early, as my housekeeper was engaged at night to partake of some friend's good cheer), and sat where I could observe without intruding on him. After a time he looked up. He was aware that somebody had entered, but could see very little of me, as I sat in the shade and he in the light. He was sad and thoughtful, and I forbore to trouble him by speaking.

Let me believe it was something better than curiosity which riveted my attention and impelled me strongly towards this gentleman. I never saw so patient and kind a face. He should have been surrounded by friends, and yet here he sat dejected and alone when all men had their friends about them. As often as he roused himself from his reverie he would fall into it again, and it was plain that, whatever were the subject of his thoughts, they were of a melancholy kind, and would not be controlled.

He was not used to solitude. I was sure of that; for I know by myself that if he had been, his manner would have been different, and he would have taken some slight interest in the arrival of another. I could not fail to mark that he had no appetite; that he tried to eat in vain; that time after time the plate was pushed away, and he relapsed into his former posture.

His mind was wandering among old Christmas days, I thought. Many of them sprung up together, not with a long gap between each, but in unbroken succession like days of the week. It was a great change to find himself for the first time (I quite settled that it *was* the first) in an empty silent room with no soul to care for. I could not help following him in imagination through crowds of pleasant faces, and then coming back to that dull place with its bough of mistletoe sickening in the gas, and sprigs of holly parched up already by a Simoom of roast and boiled. The very waiter had gone home; and his representative, a poor, lean, hungry man, was keeping Christmas in his jacket.

I grew still more interested in my friend. His dinner done, a decanter of wine was placed before him. It remained untouched for a long time, but at length with a quivering hand he filled a glass and raised it to his lips. Some tender wish to which he had been accustomed to give utterance on that day, or some beloved name that he had been used to pledge, trembled upon them at the moment. He put it down very hastily—took it up once more—again put it down—pressed his hand upon his face—yes—and tears stole down his cheeks, I am certain.

Without pausing to consider whether I did right or wrong, I stepped across the room, and sitting down beside him laid my hand gently on his arm.

'My friend,' I said, 'forgive me if I beseech you to take comfort and consolation from the lips of an old man. I will not preach to you what I have not practised, indeed. Whatever be your grief, be of a good heart—be of a good heart, pray!'

'I see that you speak earnestly,' he replied, 'and kindly I am very sure, but—'

I nodded my head to show that I understood what he would say; for I had already gathered, from a certain fixed expression in his face, and from the attention with which he watched me while I spoke, that his sense of hearing was destroyed. 'There should be a freemasonry between us,' said I, pointing from himself to me to explain my meaning; 'if not in our gray hairs, at least in our misfortunes. You see that I am but a poor cripple.'

I never felt so happy under my affliction since the trying moment of my first becoming conscious of it, as when he took my hand in his with a smile that has lighted my path in life from that day, and we sat down side by side.

This was the beginning of my friendship with the deaf gentleman; and when was ever the slight and easy service of a kind word in season repaid by such attachment and devotion as he has shown to me!

He produced a little set of tablets and a pencil to facilitate our conversation, on that our first acquaintance; and I well remember how awkward and constrained I was in writing down my share of the dialogue, and how easily he guessed my meaning before I had written half of what I had to say. He told me in a faltering voice that he had not been accustomed to be alone on that day—that it had always been a little festival with him; and seeing that I glanced at his dress in the expectation that he wore mourning, he added hastily that it was not that; if it had been he thought he could have borne it better. From that time to the present we have never touched upon this theme. Upon every return of the same day we have been together; and although we make it our annual custom to drink to each other hand in hand after dinner, and to recall with affectionate garrulity every circumstance of our first meeting, we always avoid this one as if by mutual consent.

Meantime we have gone on strengthening in our friendship and regard and forming an attachment which, I trust and believe, will only be interrupted by death, to be renewed in another existence. I scarcely know how we communicate as we do; but he has long since ceased to be deaf to me. He is frequently my companion in my walks, and even in crowded streets replies to my slightest look or gesture, as though he could read my thoughts. From the vast number of objects which pass in rapid succession before our eyes, we frequently select the same for some particular notice or remark; and when one of these little coincidences occurs, I cannot describe the pleasure which animates my friend, or the beaming countenance he will preserve for half-an-hour afterwards at least.

He is a great thinker from living so much within himself, and, having a lively imagination, has a facility of conceiving and enlarging upon odd ideas, which renders him invaluable to our little body, and greatly astonishes our two friends. His powers in this respect are much assisted by a large pipe, which he assures us once belonged to a German Student. Be this as it may, it has undoubtedly a very ancient and mysterious appearance, and is of such capacity that it takes three hours and a half to smoke it out. I have reason to believe that my barber, who is the chief authority of a knot of gossips, who congregate every evening at a small tobacconist's hard by, has related anecdotes of this pipe and the grim figures that are carved upon its bowl, at which all the smokers in the neighbourhood have stood aghast; and I know that my housekeeper, while she holds it in high veneration, has a superstitious feeling connected with it which would render her exceedingly unwilling to be left alone in its company after dark.

Whatever sorrow my dear friend has known, and whatever grief may linger in some secret corner of his heart, he is now a cheerful, placid, happy creature. Misfortune can never have fallen upon such a man but for some good purpose; and when I see its traces in his gentle nature and his earnest feeling, I am the less disposed to murmur at such trials as I may have undergone myself. With regard to the pipe, I have a theory of my own; I cannot help thinking that it is in some manner connected with the event that brought us together; for I remember that it was a long time before he even talked about it; that when he did, he grew reserved and melancholy; and that it was a long time yet before he brought it forth. I have no curiosity, however, upon this subject; for I know that it promotes his tranquillity and comfort, and I need no other inducement to regard it with my utmost favour.

Such is the deaf gentleman. I can call up his figure now, clad in sober gray, and seated in the chimney-corner. As he puffs out the smoke from his favourite pipe, he casts a look on me brimful of cordiality and friendship, and says all manner of kind and genial things in a cheerful smile; then he raises his eyes to my clock, which is just about to strike, and, glancing from it to me and back again, seems to divide his heart between us. For myself, it is not too much to say that I would gladly part with one of my poor limbs, could he but hear the old clock's voice.

Of our two friends, the first has been all his life one of that easy, wayward, truant class whom the world is accustomed to designate as nobody's enemies but their own. Bred to a profession for which he never qualified himself, and reared in the expectation of a fortune he has never inherited, he has undergone every vicissitude of which such an existence is capable. He and his younger brother, both orphans from their childhood, were educated by a wealthy relative, who taught them to expect an equal division of his property; but too indolent to court, and too honest to flatter, the elder gradually lost ground in the affections of a capricious old man, and the younger, who did not fail to improve his opportunity, now triumphs in the possession of enormous wealth. His triumph is to hoard it in solitary wretchedness, and probably to feel with the expenditure of every shilling a greater pang than the loss of his whole inheritance ever cost his brother.

Jack Redburn—he was Jack Redburn at the first little school he went to, where every other child was mastered and surnamed, and he has been Jack Redburn all his life, or he would perhaps have been a richer man by this time—has been an inmate of my house these eight years past. He is my librarian, secretary, steward, and first minister; director of all my affairs, and inspector-general of my household. He is something of a musician, something of an author, something of an actor, something of a painter, very much of a carpenter, and an extraordinary gardener, having had all his life a wonderful aptitude for learning everything that was of no use to him. He is remarkably fond of children, and is the best and kindest nurse in sickness that ever drew the breath of life. He has mixed with every grade of society, and known the utmost distress; but there never was a less selfish, a more tender- hearted, a more enthusiastic, or a more guileless man; and I dare say, if few have done less good, fewer still have done less harm in the world than he. By what chance Nature forms such whimsical jumbles I don't know; but I do know that she sends them among us very often, and that the king of the whole race is Jack Redburn.

I should be puzzled to say how old he is. His health is none of the best, and he wears a quantity of iron-gray hair, which shades his face and gives it rather a worn appearance; but we consider him quite a young fellow notwithstanding; and if a youthful spirit, surviving the roughest contact with the world, confers upon its possessor any title to be considered young, then he is a mere child. The only interruptions to his careless cheerfulness are on a wet Sunday, when he is apt to be unusually religious and solemn, and sometimes of an evening, when he has been blowing a very slow tune on the flute. On these last-named occasions he is apt to incline towards the mysterious, or the terrible. As a specimen of his powers in this mood, I refer my readers to the extract from the clock-case which follows this paper: he brought it to me not long ago at midnight, and informed me that the main incident had been suggested by a dream of the night before.

His apartments are two cheerful rooms looking towards the garden, and one of his great delights is to arrange and rearrange the furniture in these chambers, and put it in every possible variety of position. During the whole time he has been here, I do not think he has slept for two nights running with the head of his bed in the same place; and every time he moves it, is to be the last. My housekeeper was at first well-nigh distracted by these frequent changes; but she has become quite reconciled to them by degrees, and has so fallen in with his humour, that they often consult together with great gravity upon the next final alteration. Whatever his arrangements are, however, they are always a pattern of neatness; and every one of the manifold articles connected with his manifold occupations is to be found in its own particular place. Until within the last two or three years he was subject to an occasional fit (which usually came upon him in very fine weather), under the influence of which he would dress himself with peculiar care, and, going out under pretence of taking a walk, disappeared for several days together. At length, after the interval between each outbreak of this disorder had gradually grown longer and longer, it wholly disappeared; and now he seldom stirs abroad, except to stroll out a little way on a summer's evening. Whether he yet mistrusts his own constancy in this respect, and is therefore afraid to wear a coat, I know not; but we seldom see him in any other upper garment than an old spectral-looking dressing- gown, with very disproportionate pockets, full of a miscellaneous collection of odd matters, which he picks up wherever he can lay his hands upon them.

Everything that is a favourite with our friend is a favourite with us; and thus it happens that the fourth among us is Mr. Owen Miles, a most worthy gentleman, who had treated Jack with great kindness before my deaf friend and I encountered him by an accident, to which I may refer on some future occasion. Mr. Miles was once a very rich merchant; but receiving a severe shock in the death of his wife, he retired from business, and devoted himself to a quiet, unostentatious life. He is an excellent man, of thoroughly sterling character: not of quick apprehension, and not without some amusing prejudices, which I shall leave to their own development. He holds us all in profound veneration; but Jack Redburn he esteems as a kind of pleasant wonder, that he may venture to approach familiarly. He believes, not only that no man ever lived who could do so many things as Jack, but that no man ever lived who could do anything so well; and he never calls my attention to any of his ingenious proceedings, but he whispers in my ear, nudging me at the same time with his elbow: 'If he had only made it his trade, sir—if he had only made it his trade!'

They are inseparable companions; one would almost suppose that, although Mr. Miles never by any chance does anything in the way of assistance, Jack could do nothing without him. Whether he is reading, writing, painting, carpentering, gardening, flute-playing, or what not, there is Mr. Miles beside him, buttoned up to the chin in his blue coat, and looking on with a face of incredulous delight, as though he could not credit the testimony of his own senses, and had a misgiving that no man could be so clever but in a dream.

These are my friends; I have now introduced myself and them.

THE CLOCK-CASE. A CONFESSION FOUND IN A PRISON IN THE TIME OF CHARLES THE SECOND

I held a lieutenant's commission in his Majesty's army, and served abroad in the campaigns of 1677 and 1678. The treaty of Nimeguen being concluded, I returned home, and retiring from the service, withdrew to a small estate lying a few miles east of London, which I had recently acquired in right of my wife.

This is the last night I have to live, and I will set down the naked truth without disguise. I was never a brave man, and had always been from my childhood of a secret, sullen, distrustful nature. I speak of myself as if I had passed from the world; for while I write this, my grave is digging, and my name is written in the black-book of death.

Soon after my return to England, my only brother was seized with mortal illness. This circumstance gave me slight or no pain; for since we had been men, we had associated but very little together. He was open-hearted and generous, handsomer than I, more accomplished, and generally beloved. Those who sought my acquaintance abroad or at home, because they were friends of his, seldom attached themselves to me long, and would usually say, in our first conversation, that they were surprised to find two brothers so unlike in their manners and appearance. It was my habit to lead them on to this avowal; for I knew what comparisons they must draw between us; and having a rankling envy in my heart, I sought to justify it to myself.

We had married two sisters. This additional tie between us, as it may appear to some, only estranged us the more. His wife knew me well. I never struggled with any secret jealousy or gall when she was present but that woman knew it as well as I did. I never raised my eyes at such times but I found hers fixed upon me; I never bent them on the ground or looked another way but I felt that she overlooked me always. It was an inexpressible relief to me when we quarrelled, and a greater relief still when I heard abroad that she was dead. It seems to me now as if some strange and terrible foreshadowing of what has happened since must have hung over us then. I was afraid of her; she haunted me; her fixed and steady look comes back upon me now, like the memory of a dark dream, and makes my blood run cold.

She died shortly after giving birth to a child—a boy. When my brother knew that all hope of his own recovery was past, he called my wife to his bedside, and confided this orphan, a child of four years old, to her protection. He bequeathed to him all the property he had, and willed that, in case of his child's death, it should pass to my wife, as the only acknowledgment he could make her for her care and love. He exchanged a few brotherly words with me, deploring our long separation; and being exhausted, fell into a slumber, from which he never awoke.

We had no children; and as there had been a strong affection between the sisters, and my wife had almost supplied the place of a mother to this boy, she loved him as if he had been her own. The child was ardently attached to her; but he was his mother's image in face and spirit, and always mistrusted me.

I can scarcely fix the date when the feeling first came upon me; but I soon began to be uneasy when this child was by. I never roused myself from some moody train of thought but I marked him looking at me; not with mere childish wonder, but with something of the purpose and meaning that I had so often noted in his mother. It was no effort of my fancy, founded on close resemblance of feature and expression. I never could look the boy down. He feared me, but seemed by some instinct to despise me while he did so; and even when he drew back beneath my gaze—as he would when we were alone, to get nearer to the door—he would keep his bright eyes upon me still.

Perhaps I hide the truth from myself, but I do not think that, when this began, I meditated to do him any wrong. I may have thought how serviceable his inheritance would be to us, and may have wished him dead; but I believe I had no thought of compassing his death. Neither did the idea come upon me at once, but by very slow degrees, presenting itself at first in dim shapes at a very great distance, as men may think of an earthquake or the last day; then drawing nearer and nearer, and losing something of its horror and improbability; then coming to be part and parcel—nay nearly the whole sum and substance—of my daily thoughts, and resolving itself into a question of means and safety; not of doing or abstaining from the deed.

While this was going on within me, I never could bear that the child should see me looking at him, and yet I was under a fascination which made it a kind of business with me to contemplate his slight and fragile figure and think how easily it might be done. Sometimes I would steal up-stairs and watch him as he slept; but usually I hovered in the garden near the window of the room in which he learnt his little tasks; and there, as he sat upon a low seat beside my wife, I would peer at him for hours together from behind a tree; starting, like the guilty wretch I was, at every rustling of a leaf, and still gliding back to look and start again.

Hard by our cottage, but quite out of sight, and (if there were any wind astir) of hearing too, was a deep sheet of water. I spent days in shaping with my pocket-knife a rough model of a boat, which I finished at last and dropped in the child's way. Then I withdrew to a secret place, which he must pass if he stole away alone to swim this bauble, and lurked there for his coming. He came neither that day nor the next, though I waited from noon till nightfall. I was sure that I had him in my net, for I had heard him prattling of the toy, and knew that in his infant pleasure he kept it by his side in bed. I felt no weariness or fatigue, but waited patiently, and on the third day he passed me, running joyously along, with his silken hair streaming in the wind, and he singing—God have mercy upon me!—singing a merry ballad,—who could hardly lisp the words.

I stole down after him, creeping under certain shrubs which grow in that place, and none but devils know with what terror I, a strong, full-grown man, tracked the footsteps of that baby as he approached the water's brink. I was close upon him, had sunk upon my knee and raised my hand to thrust him in, when he saw my shadow in the stream and turned him round.

His mother's ghost was looking from his eyes. The sun burst forth from behind a cloud; it shone in the bright sky, the glistening earth, the clear water, the sparkling drops of rain upon the leaves. There were eyes in everything. The whole great universe of light was there to see the murder done. I know not what he said; he came of bold and manly blood, and, child as he was, he did not crouch or fawn upon me. I heard him cry that he would try to love me,—not that he did,—and then I saw him running back towards the house. The next I saw was my own sword naked in my hand, and he lying at my feet stark dead,—dabbled here and there with blood, but otherwise no different from what I had seen him in his sleep—in the same attitude too, with his cheek resting upon his little hand.

I took him in my arms and laid him—very gently now that he was dead—in a thicket. My wife was from home that day, and would not return until the next. Our bedroom window, the only sleeping-room on that side of the house, was but a few feet from the ground, and I resolved to descend from it at night and bury him in the garden. I had no thought that I had failed in my design, no thought that the water would be dragged and nothing found, that the money must now lie waste, since I must encourage the idea that the child was lost or stolen. All my thoughts were bound up and knotted together in the one absorbing necessity of hiding what I had done.

How I felt when they came to tell me that the child was missing, when I ordered scouts in all directions, when I gasped and trembled at every one's approach, no tongue can tell or mind of man conceive. I buried him that night. When I parted the boughs and looked into the dark thicket, there was a glow-worm shining like the visible spirit of God upon the murdered child. I glanced down into his grave when I had placed him there, and still it gleamed upon his breast; an eye of fire looking up to Heaven in supplication to the stars that watched me at my work.

I had to meet my wife, and break the news, and give her hope that the child would soon be found. All this I did,—with some appearance, I suppose, of being sincere, for I was the object of no suspicion. This done, I sat at the bedroom window all day long, and watched the spot where the dreadful secret lay.

It was in a piece of ground which had been dug up to be newly turfed, and which I had chosen on that account, as the traces of my spade were less likely to attract attention. The men who laid down the grass must have thought me mad. I called to them continually to expedite their work, ran out and worked beside them, trod down the earth with my feet, and hurried them with frantic eagerness. They had finished their task before night, and then I thought myself comparatively safe.

I slept,—not as men do who awake refreshed and cheerful, but I did sleep, passing from vague and shadowy dreams of being hunted down, to visions of the plot of grass, through which now a hand, and now a foot, and now the head itself was starting out. At this point I always woke and stole to the window, to make sure that it was not really so. That done, I crept to bed again; and thus I spent the night in fits and starts, getting up and lying down full twenty times, and dreaming the same dream over and over again,—which was far worse than lying awake, for every dream had a whole night's suffering of its own. Once I thought the child was alive, and that I had never tried to kill him. To wake from that dream was the most dreadful agony of all.

The next day I sat at the window again, never once taking my eyes from the place, which, although it was covered by the grass, was as plain to me—its shape, its size, its depth, its jagged sides, and all—as if it had been open to the light of day. When a servant walked across it, I felt as if he must sink in; when he had passed, I looked to see that his feet had not worn the edges. If a bird lighted there, I was in terror lest by some tremendous interposition it should be instrumental in the discovery; if a breath of air sighed across it, to me it whispered murder. There was not a sight or a sound—how ordinary, mean, or unimportant soever—but was fraught with fear. And in this state of ceaseless watching I spent three days.

On the fourth there came to the gate one who had served with me abroad, accompanied by a brother officer of his whom I had never seen. I felt that I could not bear to be out of sight of the place. It was a summer evening, and I bade my people take a table and a flask of wine into the garden. Then I sat down *with my chair upon the grave*, and being assured that nobody could disturb it now without my knowledge, tried to drink and talk.

They hoped that my wife was well,—that she was not obliged to keep her chamber,—that they had not frightened her away. What could I do but tell them with a faltering tongue about the child? The officer whom I did not know was a down-looking man, and kept his eyes upon the ground while I was speaking. Even that terrified me. I could not divest myself of the idea that he saw something there which caused him to suspect the truth. I asked him hurriedly if he supposed that—and stopped. 'That the child has been murdered?' said he, looking mildly at me: 'O no! what could a man gain by murdering a poor child?' I could have told him what a man gained by such a deed, no one better: but I held my peace and shivered as with an ague.

Mistaking my emotion, they were endeavouring to cheer me with the hope that the boy would certainly be found,—great cheer that was for me!—when we heard a low deep howl, and presently there sprung over the wall two great dogs, who, bounding into the garden, repeated the baying sound we had heard before.

'Bloodhounds!' cried my visitors.

What need to tell me that! I had never seen one of that kind in all my life, but I knew what they were and for what purpose they had come. I grasped the elbows of my chair, and neither spoke nor moved.

'They are of the genuine breed,' said the man whom I had known abroad, 'and being out for exercise have no doubt escaped from their keeper.'

Both he and his friend turned to look at the dogs, who with their noses to the ground moved restlessly about, running to and fro, and up and down, and across, and round in circles, careering about like wild things, and all this time taking no notice of us, but ever and again repeating the yell we had heard already, then dropping their noses to the ground again and tracking earnestly here and there. They now began to snuff the earth more eagerly than they had done yet, and although they were still very restless, no longer beat about in such wide circuits, but kept near to one spot, and constantly diminished the distance between themselves and me.

At last they came up close to the great chair on which I sat, and raising their frightful howl once more, tried to tear away the wooden rails that kept them from the ground beneath. I saw how I looked, in the faces of the two who were with me.

'They scent some prey,' said they, both together.

'They scent no prey!' cried I.

'In Heaven's name, move!' said the one I knew, very earnestly, 'or you will be torn to pieces.'

'Let them tear me from limb to limb, I'll never leave this place!' cried I. 'Are dogs to hurry men to shameful deaths? Hew them down, cut them in pieces.'

'There is some foul mystery here!' said the officer whom I did not know, drawing his sword. 'In King Charles's name, assist me to secure this man.'

They both set upon me and forced me away, though I fought and bit and caught at them like a madman. After a struggle, they got me quietly between them; and then, my God! I saw the angry dogs tearing at the earth and throwing it up into the air like water.

What more have I to tell? That I fell upon my knees, and with chattering teeth confessed the truth, and prayed to be forgiven. That I have since denied, and now confess to it again. That I have been tried for the crime, found guilty, and sentenced. That I have not the courage to anticipate my doom, or to bear up manfully against it. That I have no compassion, no consolation, no hope, no friend. That my wife has happily lost for the time those faculties which would enable her to know my misery or hers. That I am alone in this stone dungeon with my evil spirit, and that I die to- morrow.

CORRESPONDENCE

Master Humphrey has been favoured with the following letter written on strongly-scented paper, and sealed in light-blue wax with the representation of two very plump doves interchanging beaks. It does not commence with any of the usual forms of address, but begins as is here set forth.

'Bath,
Wednesday night.

Heavens! into what an indiscretion do I suffer myself to be betrayed! To address these faltering lines to a total stranger, and that stranger one of a conflicting sex! —and yet I am precipitated into the abyss, and have no power of self-snatchation (forgive me if I coin that phrase) from the yawning gulf before me.

Yes, I am writing to a man; but let me not think of that, for madness is in the thought. You will understand my feelings? O yes, I am sure you will; and you will respect them too, and not despise them,—will you?

Let me be calm. That portrait,—smiling as once he smiled on me; that cane,—dangling as I have seen it dangle from his hand I know not how oft; those legs that have glided through my nightly dreams and never stopped to speak; the perfectly gentlemanly, though false original,—can I be mistaken? O no, no.

Let me be calmer yet; I would be calm as coffins. You have published a letter from one whose likeness is engraved, but whose name (and wherefore?) is suppressed. Shall I breathe that name! Is it—but why ask when my heart tells me too truly that it is!

I would not upbraid him with his treachery; I would not remind him of those times when he plighted the most eloquent of vows, and procured from me a small pecuniary accommodation; and yet I would see him—see him did I say—*him*—alas! such is woman's nature. For as the poet beautifully says—but you will already have anticipated the sentiment. Is it not sweet? O yes!

It was in this city (hallowed by the recollection) that I met him first; and assuredly if mortal happiness be recorded anywhere, then those rubbers with their three-and sixpenny points are scored on tablets of celestial brass. He always held an honour—generally two. On that eventful night we stood at eight. He raised his eyes (luminous in their seductive sweetness) to my agitated face. '*Can* you?' said he, with peculiar meaning. I felt the gentle pressure of his foot on mine; our corns throbbed in unison. '*Can* you?' he said again; and every lineament of his expressive countenance added the words 'resist me?' I murmured 'No,' and fainted.

They said, when I recovered, it was the weather. I said it was the nutmeg in the negus. How little did they suspect the truth! How little did they guess the deep mysterious meaning of that inquiry! He called next morning on his knees; I do not mean to say that he actually came in that position to the house-door, but that he went down upon those joints directly the servant had retired. He brought some verses in his hat, which he said were original, but which I have since found were Milton's; likewise a little bottle labelled laudanum; also a pistol and a sword-stick. He drew the latter, uncorked the former, and clicked the trigger of the pocket fire-arm. He had come, he said, to conquer or to die. He did not die. He wrested from me an avowal of my love, and let off the pistol out of a back window previous to partaking of a slight repast.

Faithless, inconstant man! How many ages seem to have elapsed since his unaccountable and perfidious disappearance! Could I still forgive him both that and the borrowed lucre that he promised to pay next week! Could I spurn him from my feet if he approached in penitence, and with a matrimonial object! Would the blandishing enchanter still weave his spells around me, or should I burst them all and turn away in coldness! I dare not trust my weakness with the thought.

My brain is in a whirl again. You know his address, his occupations, his mode of life,—are acquainted, perhaps, with his inmost thoughts. You are a humane and philanthropic character; reveal all you know—all; but especially the street and number of his lodgings. The post is departing, the bellman rings,—pray Heaven it be not the knell of love and hope to BELINDA.

P.S. Pardon the wanderings of a bad pen and a distracted mind. Address to the Post-office. The bellman, rendered impatient by delay, is ringing dreadfully in the passage.

P.P.S. I open this to say that the bellman is gone, and that you must not expect it till the next post; so don't be surprised when you don't get it.'

Master Humphrey does not feel himself at liberty to furnish his fair correspondent with the address of the gentleman in question, but he publishes her letter as a public appeal to his faith and gallantry.

CHAPTER III—MASTER HUMPHREY'S VISITOR

WHEN I am in a thoughtful mood, I often succeed in diverting the current of some mournful reflections, by conjuring up a number of fanciful associations with the objects that surround me, and dwelling upon the scenes and characters they suggest.

I have been led by this habit to assign to every room in my house and every old staring portrait on its walls a separate interest of its own. Thus, I am persuaded that a stately dame, terrible to behold in her rigid modesty, who hangs above the chimney-piece of my bedroom, is the former lady of the mansion. In the courtyard below is a stone face of surpassing ugliness, which I have somehow—in a kind of jealousy, I am afraid—associated with her husband. Above my study is a little room with ivy peeping through the lattice, from which I bring their daughter, a lovely girl of eighteen or nineteen years of age, and dutiful in all respects save one, that one being her devoted attachment to a young gentleman on the stairs, whose grandmother (degraded to a disused laundry in the garden) piques herself upon an old family quarrel, and is the implacable enemy of their love. With such materials as these I work out many a little drama, whose chief merit is, that I can bring it to a happy end at will. I have so many of them on hand, that if on my return home one of these evenings I were to find some bluff old wight of two centuries ago comfortably seated in my easy chair, and a lovelorn damsel vainly appealing to his heart, and leaning her white arm upon my clock itself, I verily believe I should only express my surprise that they had kept me waiting so long, and never honoured me with a call before.

I was in such a mood as this, sitting in my garden yesterday morning under the shade of a favourite tree, revelling in all the bloom and brightness about me, and feeling every sense of hope and enjoyment quickened by this most beautiful season of Spring, when my meditations were interrupted by the unexpected appearance of my barber at the end of the walk, who I immediately saw was coming towards me with a hasty step that betokened something remarkable.

My barber is at all times a very brisk, bustling, active little man,—for he is, as it were, chubby all over, without being stout or unwieldy,—but yesterday his alacrity was so very uncommon that it quite took me by surprise. For could I fail to observe when he came up to me that his gray eyes were twinkling in a most extraordinary manner, that his little red nose was in an unusual glow, that every line in his round bright face was twisted and curved into an expression of pleased surprise, and that his whole countenance was radiant with glee? I was still more surprised to see my housekeeper, who usually preserves a very staid air, and stands somewhat upon her dignity, peeping round the hedge at the bottom of the walk, and exchanging nods and smiles with the barber, who twice or thrice looked over his shoulder for that purpose. I could conceive no announcement to which these appearances could be the prelude, unless it were that they had married each other that morning.

I was, consequently, a little disappointed when it only came out that there was a gentleman in the house who wished to speak with me.

'And who is it?' said I.

The barber, with his face screwed up still tighter than before, replied that the gentleman would not send his name, but wished to see me. I pondered for a moment, wondering who this visitor might be, and I remarked that he embraced the opportunity of exchanging another nod with the housekeeper, who still lingered in the distance.

'Well!' said I, 'bid the gentleman come here.'

This seemed to be the consummation of the barber's hopes, for he turned sharp round, and actually ran away.

Now, my sight is not very good at a distance, and therefore when the gentleman first appeared in the walk, I was not quite clear whether he was a stranger to me or otherwise. He was an elderly gentleman, but came tripping along in the pleasantest manner conceivable, avoiding the garden-roller and the borders of the beds with inimitable dexterity, picking his way among the flower-pots, and smiling with unspeakable good humour. Before he was half-way up the walk he began to salute me; then I thought I knew him; but when he came towards me with his hat in his hand, the sun shining on his bald head, his bland face, his bright spectacles, his fawn- coloured tights, and his black gaiters,—then my heart warmed towards him, and I felt quite certain that it was Mr. Pickwick.

'My dear sir,' said that gentleman as I rose to receive him, 'pray be seated. Pray sit down. Now, do not stand on my account. I must insist upon it, really.' With these words Mr. Pickwick gently pressed me down into my seat, and taking my hand in his, shook it again and again with a warmth of manner perfectly irresistible. I endeavoured to express in my welcome something of that heartiness and pleasure which the sight of him awakened, and made him sit down beside me. All this time he kept alternately releasing my hand and grasping it again, and surveying me through his spectacles with such a beaming countenance as I never till then beheld.

'You knew me directly!' said Mr. Pickwick. 'What a pleasure it is to think that you knew me directly!'

I remarked that I had read his adventures very often, and his features were quite familiar to me from the published portraits. As I thought it a good opportunity of adverting to the circumstance, I condoled with him upon the various libels on his character which had found their way into print. Mr. Pickwick shook his head, and for a moment looked very indignant, but smiling again directly, added that no doubt I was acquainted with Cervantes's introduction to the second part of Don Quixote, and that it fully expressed his sentiments on the subject.

'But now,' said Mr. Pickwick, 'don't you wonder how I found you out?'

'I shall never wonder, and, with your good leave, never know,' said I, smiling in my turn. 'It is enough for me that you give me this gratification. I have not the least desire that you should tell me by what means I have obtained it.'

'You are very kind,' returned Mr. Pickwick, shaking me by the hand again; 'you are so exactly what I expected! But for what particular purpose do you think I have sought you, my dear sir? Now what *do* you think I have come for?'

Mr. Pickwick put this question as though he were persuaded that it was morally impossible that I could by any means divine the deep purpose of his visit, and that it must be hidden from all human ken. Therefore, although I was rejoiced to think that I had anticipated his drift, I feigned to be quite ignorant of it, and after a brief consideration shook my head despairingly.

'What should you say,' said Mr. Pickwick, laying the forefinger of his left hand upon my coat-sleeve, and looking at me with his head thrown back, and a little on one side,—'what should you say if I confessed that after reading your account of yourself and your little society, I had come here, a humble candidate for one of those empty chairs?'

'I should say,' I returned, 'that I know of only one circumstance which could still further endear that little society to me, and that would be the associating with it my old friend,—for you must let me call you so,—my old friend, Mr. Pickwick.'

As I made him this answer every feature of Mr. Pickwick's face fused itself into one all-pervading expression of delight. After shaking me heartily by both hands at once, he patted me gently on the back, and then—I well understood why—coloured up to the eyes, and hoped with great earnestness of manner that he had not hurt me.

If he had, I would have been content that he should have repeated the offence a hundred times rather than suppose so; but as he had not, I had no difficulty in changing the subject by making an inquiry which had been upon my lips twenty times already.

'You have not told me,' said I, 'anything about Sam Weller.'

'O! Sam,' replied Mr. Pickwick, 'is the same as ever. The same true, faithful fellow that he ever was. What should I tell you about Sam, my dear sir, except that he is more indispensable to my happiness and comfort every day of my life?'

'And Mr. Weller senior?' said I.

'Old Mr. Weller,' returned Mr. Pickwick, 'is in no respect more altered than Sam, unless it be that he is a little more opinionated than he was formerly, and perhaps at times more talkative. He spends a good deal of his time now in our neighbourhood, and has so constituted himself a part of my bodyguard, that when I ask permission for Sam to have a seat in your kitchen on clock nights (supposing your three friends think me worthy to fill one of the chairs), I am afraid I must often include Mr. Weller too.'

I very readily pledged myself to give both Sam and his father a free admission to my house at all hours and seasons, and this point settled, we fell into a lengthy conversation which was carried on with as little reserve on both sides as if we had been intimate friends from our youth, and which conveyed to me the comfortable assurance that Mr. Pickwick's buoyancy of spirit, and indeed all his old cheerful characteristics, were wholly unimpaired. As he had spoken of the consent of my friends as being yet in abeyance, I repeatedly assured him that his proposal was certain to receive their most joyful sanction, and several times entreated that he would give me leave to introduce him to Jack Redburn and Mr. Miles (who were near at hand) without further ceremony.

To this proposal, however, Mr. Pickwick's delicacy would by no means allow him to accede, for he urged that his eligibility must be formally discussed, and that, until this had been done, he could not think of obtruding himself further. The utmost I could obtain from him was a promise that he would attend upon our next night of meeting, that I might have the pleasure of presenting him immediately on his election.

Mr. Pickwick, having with many blushes placed in my hands a small roll of paper, which he termed his 'qualification,' put a great many questions to me touching my friends, and particularly Jack Redburn, whom he repeatedly termed 'a fine fellow,' and in whose favour I could see he was strongly predisposed. When I had satisfied him on these points, I took him up into my room, that he might make acquaintance with the old chamber which is our place of meeting.

'And this,' said Mr. Pickwick, stopping short, 'is the clock! Dear me! And this is really the old clock!'

I thought he would never have come away from it. After advancing towards it softly, and laying his hand upon it with as much respect and as many smiling looks as if it were alive, he set himself to consider it in every possible direction, now mounting on a chair to look at the top, now going down upon his knees to examine the bottom, now surveying the sides with his spectacles almost touching the case, and now trying to peep between it and the wall to get a slight view of the back. Then he would retire a pace or two and look up at the dial to see it go, and then draw near again and stand with his head on one side to hear it tick: never failing to glance towards me at intervals of a few seconds each, and nod his head with such complacent gratification as I am quite unable to describe. His admiration was not confined to the clock either, but extended itself to every article in the room; and really, when he had gone through them every one, and at last sat himself down in all the six chairs, one after another, to try how they felt, I never saw such a picture of good-humour and happiness as he presented, from the top of his shining head down to the very last button of his gaiters.

I should have been well pleased, and should have had the utmost enjoyment of his company, if he had remained with me all day, but my favourite, striking the hour, reminded him that he must take his leave. I could not forbear telling him once more how glad he had made me, and we shook hands all the way down-stairs.

We had no sooner arrived in the Hall than my housekeeper, gliding out of her little room (she had changed her gown and cap, I observed), greeted Mr. Pickwick with her best smile and courtesy; and the barber, feigning to be accidentally passing on his way out, made him a vast number of bows. When the housekeeper courtesied, Mr. Pickwick bowed with the utmost politeness, and when he bowed, the housekeeper courtesied again; between the housekeeper and the barber, I should say that Mr. Pickwick faced about and bowed with undiminished affability fifty times at least.

I saw him to the door; an omnibus was at the moment passing the corner of the lane, which Mr. Pickwick hailed and ran after with extraordinary nimbleness. When he had got about half-way, he turned his head, and seeing that I was still looking after him and that I waved my hand, stopped, evidently irresolute whether to come back and shake hands again, or to go on. The man behind the omnibus shouted, and Mr. Pickwick ran a little way towards him: then he looked round at me, and ran a little way back again. Then there was another shout, and he turned round once more and ran the other way. After several of these vibrations, the man settled the question by taking Mr. Pickwick by the arm and putting him into the carriage; but his last action was to let down the window and wave his hat to me as it drove off.

I lost no time in opening the parcel he had left with me. The following were its contents:—

MR. PICKWICK'S TALE

A good many years have passed away since old John Podgers lived in the town of Windsor, where he was born, and where, in course of time, he came to be comfortably and snugly buried. You may be sure that in the time of King James the First, Windsor was a very quaint queer old town, and you may take it upon my authority that John Podgers was a very quaint queer old fellow; consequently he and Windsor fitted each other to a nicety, and seldom parted company even for half a day.

John Podgers was broad, sturdy, Dutch-built, short, and a very hard eater, as men of his figure often are. Being a hard sleeper likewise, he divided his time pretty equally between these two recreations, always falling asleep when he had done eating, and always taking another turn at the trencher when he had done sleeping, by which means he grew more corpulent and more drowsy every day of his life. Indeed it used to be currently reported that when he sauntered up and down the sunny side of the street before dinner (as he never failed to do in fair weather), he enjoyed his soundest nap; but many people held this to be a fiction, as he had several times been seen to look after fat oxen on market-days, and had even been heard, by persons of good credit and reputation, to chuckle at the sight, and say to himself with great glee, 'Live beef, live beef!' It was upon this evidence that the wisest people in Windsor (beginning with the local authorities of course) held that John Podgers was a man of strong, sound sense, not what is called smart, perhaps, and it might be of a rather lazy and apoplectic turn, but still a man of solid parts, and one who meant much more than he cared to show. This impression was confirmed by a very dignified way he had of shaking his head and imparting, at the same time, a pendulous motion to his double chin; in short, he passed for one of those people who, being plunged into the Thames, would make no vain efforts to set it afire, but would straightway flop down to the bottom with a deal of gravity, and be highly respected in consequence by all good men.

Being well to do in the world, and a peaceful widower,—having a great appetite, which, as he could afford to gratify it, was a luxury and no inconvenience, and a power of going to sleep, which, as he had no occasion to keep awake, was a most enviable faculty,—you will readily suppose that John Podgers was a happy man. But appearances are often deceptive when they least seem so, and the truth is that, notwithstanding his extreme sleekness, he was rendered uneasy in his mind and exceedingly uncomfortable by a constant apprehension that beset him night and day.

You know very well that in those times there flourished divers evil old women who, under the name of Witches, spread great disorder through the land, and inflicted various dismal tortures upon Christian men; sticking pins and needles into them when they least expected it, and causing them to walk in the air with their feet upwards, to the great terror of their wives and families, who were naturally very much disconcerted when the master of the house unexpectedly came home, knocking at the door with his heels and combing his hair on the scraper. These were their commonest pranks, but they every day played a hundred others, of which none were less objectionable, and many were much more so, being improper besides; the result was that vengeance was denounced against all old women, with whom even the king himself had no sympathy (as he certainly ought to have had), for with his own most Gracious hand he penned a most Gracious consignment of them to everlasting wrath, and devised most Gracious means for their confusion and slaughter, in virtue whereof scarcely a day passed but one witch at the least was most graciously hanged, drowned, or roasted in some part of his dominions. Still the press teemed with strange and terrible news from the North or the South, or the East or the West, relative to witches and their unhappy victims in some corner of the country, and the Public's hair stood on end to that degree that it lifted its hat off its head, and made its face pale with terror.

You may believe that the little town of Windsor did not escape the general contagion. The inhabitants boiled a witch on the king's birthday and sent a bottle of the broth to court, with a dutiful address expressive of their loyalty. The king, being rather frightened by the present, piously bestowed it upon the Archbishop of Canterbury, and returned an answer to the address, wherein he gave them golden rules for discovering witches, and laid great stress upon certain protecting charms, and especially horseshoes. Immediately the towns-people went to work nailing up horseshoes over every door, and so many anxious parents apprenticed their children to farriers to keep them out of harm's way, that it became quite a genteel trade, and flourished exceedingly.

In the midst of all this bustle John Podgers ate and slept as usual, but shook his head a great deal oftener than was his custom, and was observed to look at the oxen less, and at the old women more. He had a little shelf put up in his sitting-room, whereon was displayed, in a row which grew longer every week, all the witchcraft literature of the time; he grew learned in charms and exorcisms, hinted at certain questionable females on broomsticks whom he had seen from his chamber window, riding in the air at night, and was in constant terror of being bewitched. At length, from perpetually dwelling upon this one idea, which, being alone in his head, had all its own way, the fear of witches became the single passion of his life. He, who up to that time had never known what it was to dream, began to have visions of witches whenever he fell asleep; waking, they were incessantly present to his imagination likewise; and, sleeping or waking, he had not a moment's peace. He began to set witch-traps in the highway, and was often seen lying in wait round the corner for hours together, to watch their effect. These engines were of simple construction, usually consisting of two straws disposed in the form of a cross, or a piece of a Bible cover with a pinch of salt upon it; but they were infallible, and if an old woman chanced to stumble over them (as not unfrequently happened, the chosen spot being a broken and stony place), John started from a doze, pounced out upon her, and hung round her neck till assistance arrived, when she was immediately carried away and drowned. By dint of constantly inveigling old ladies and disposing of them in this summary manner, he acquired the reputation of a great public character; and as he received no harm in these pursuits beyond a scratched face or so, he came, in the course of time, to be considered witch-proof.

There was but one person who entertained the least doubt of John Podgers's gifts, and that person was his own nephew, a wild, roving young fellow of twenty who had been brought up in his uncle's house and lived there still,—that is to say, when he was at home, which was not as often as it might have been. As he was an apt scholar, it was he who read aloud every fresh piece of strange and terrible intelligence that John Podgers bought; and this he always did of an evening in the little porch in front of the house, round which the neighbours would flock in crowds to hear the direful news,—for people like to be frightened, and when they can be frightened for nothing and at another man's expense, they like it all the better.

One fine midsummer evening, a group of persons were gathered in this place, listening intently to Will Marks (that was the nephew's name), as with his cap very much on one side, his arm coiled slyly round the waist of a pretty girl who sat beside him, and his face screwed into a comical expression intended to represent extreme gravity, he read—with Heaven knows how many embellishments of his own—a dismal account of a gentleman down in Northamptonshire under the influence of witchcraft and taken forcible possession of by the Devil, who was playing his very self with him. John Podgers, in a high sugar-loaf hat and short cloak, filled the opposite seat, and surveyed the auditory with a look of mingled pride and horror very edifying to see; while the hearers, with their heads thrust forward and their mouths open, listened and trembled, and hoped there was a great deal more to come. Sometimes Will stopped for an instant to look round upon his eager audience, and then, with a more comical expression of face than before and a settling of himself comfortably, which included a squeeze of the young lady before mentioned, he launched into some new wonder surpassing all the others.

The setting sun shed his last golden rays upon this little party, who, absorbed in their present occupation, took no heed of the approach of night, or the glory in which the day went down, when the sound of a horse, approaching at a good round trot, invading the silence of the hour, caused the reader to make a sudden stop, and the listeners to raise their heads in wonder. Nor was their wonder diminished when a horseman dashed up to the porch, and abruptly checking his steed, inquired where one John Podgers dwelt.

'Here!' cried a dozen voices, while a dozen hands pointed out sturdy John, still basking in the terrors of the pamphlet.

The rider, giving his bridle to one of those who surrounded him, dismounted, and approached John, hat in hand, but with great haste.

'Whence come ye?' said John.

'From Kingston, master.'

'And wherefore?'

'On most pressing business.'

'Of what nature?'

'Witchcraft.'

Witchcraft! Everybody looked aghast at the breathless messenger, and the breathless messenger looked equally aghast at everybody—except Will Marks, who, finding himself unobserved, not only squeezed the young lady again, but kissed her twice. Surely he must have been bewitched himself, or he never could have done it—and the young lady too, or she never would have let him.

'Witchcraft!' cried Will, drowning the sound of his last kiss, which was rather a loud one.

The messenger turned towards him, and with a frown repeated the word more solemnly than before; then told his errand, which was, in brief, that the people of Kingston had been greatly terrified for some nights past by hideous revels, held by witches beneath the gibbet within a mile of the town, and related and deposed to by chance wayfarers who had passed within ear-shot of the spot; that the sound of their voices in their wild orgies had been plainly heard by many persons; that three old women laboured under strong suspicion, and that precedents had been consulted and solemn council had, and it was found that to identify the hags some single person must watch upon the spot alone; that no single person had the courage to perform the task; and that he had been despatched express to solicit John Podgers to undertake it that very night, as being a man of great renown, who bore a charmed life, and was proof against unholy spells.

John received this communication with much composure, and said in a few words, that it would have afforded him inexpressible pleasure to do the Kingston people so slight a service, if it were not for his unfortunate propensity to fall asleep, which no man regretted more than himself upon the present occasion, but which quite settled the question. Nevertheless, he said, there WAS a gentleman present (and here he looked very hard at a tall farrier), who, having been engaged all his life in the manufacture of horseshoes, must be quite invulnerable to the power of witches, and who, he had no doubt, from his own reputation for bravery and good-nature, would readily accept the commission. The farrier politely thanked him for his good opinion, which it would always be his study to deserve, but added that, with regard to the present little matter, he couldn't think of it on any account, as his departing on such an errand would certainly occasion the instant death of his wife, to whom, as they all knew, he was tenderly attached. Now, so far from this circumstance being notorious, everybody had suspected the reverse, as the farrier was in the habit of beating his lady rather more than tender husbands usually do; all the married men present, however, applauded his resolution with great vehemence, and one and all declared that they would stop at home and die if needful (which happily it was not) in defence of their lawful partners.

This burst of enthusiasm over, they began to look, as by one consent, toward Will Marks, who, with his cap more on one side than ever, sat watching the proceedings with extraordinary unconcern. He had never been heard openly to express his disbelief in witches, but had often cut such jokes at their expense as left it to be inferred; publicly stating on several occasions that he considered a broomstick an inconvenient charger, and one especially unsuited to the dignity of the female character, and indulging in other free remarks of the same tendency, to the great amusement of his wild companions.

As they looked at Will they began to whisper and murmur among themselves, and at length one man cried, 'Why don't you ask Will Marks?'

As this was what everybody had been thinking of, they all took up the word, and cried in concert, 'Ah! why don't you ask Will?'

'*He* don't care,' said the farrier.

'Not he,' added another voice in the crowd.

'He don't believe in it, you know,' sneered a little man with a yellow face and a taunting nose and chin, which he thrust out from under the arm of a long man before him.

'Besides,' said a red-faced gentleman with a gruff voice, 'he's a single man.'

'That's the point!' said the farrier; and all the married men murmured, ah! that was it, and they only wished they were single themselves; they would show him what spirit was, very soon.

The messenger looked towards Will Marks beseechingly.

'It will be a wet night, friend, and my gray nag is tired after yesterday's work—'

Here there was a general titter.

'But,' resumed Will, looking about him with a smile, 'if nobody else puts in a better claim to go, for the credit of the town I am your man, and I would be, if I had to go afoot. In five minutes I shall be in the saddle, unless I am depriving any worthy gentleman here of the honour of the adventure, which I wouldn't do for the world.'

But here arose a double difficulty, for not only did John Podgers combat the resolution with all the words he had, which were not many, but the young lady combated it too with all the tears she had, which were very many indeed. Will, however, being inflexible, parried his uncle's objections with a joke, and coaxed the young lady into a smile in three short whispers. As it was plain that he set his mind upon it, and would go, John Podgers offered him a few first-rate charms out of his own pocket, which he dutifully declined to accept; and the young lady gave him a kiss, which he also returned.

'You see what a rare thing it is to be married,' said Will, 'and how careful and considerate all these husbands are. There's not a man among them but his heart is leaping to forestall me in this adventure, and yet a strong sense of duty keeps him back. The husbands in this one little town are a pattern to the world, and so must the wives be too, for that matter, or they could never boast half the influence they have!'

Waiting for no reply to this sarcasm, he snapped his fingers and withdrew into the house, and thence into the stable, while some busied themselves in refreshing the messenger, and others in baiting his steed. In less than the specified time he returned by another way, with a good cloak hanging over his arm, a good sword girded by his side, and leading his good horse caparisoned for the journey.

'Now,' said Will, leaping into the saddle at a bound, 'up and away. Upon your mettle, friend, and push on. Good night!'

He kissed his hand to the girl, nodded to his drowsy uncle, waved his cap to the rest—and off they flew pell-mell, as if all the witches in England were in their horses' legs. They were out of sight in a minute.

The men who were left behind shook their heads doubtfully, stroked their chins, and shook their heads again. The farrier said that certainly Will Marks was a good horseman, nobody should ever say he denied that: but he was rash, very rash, and there was no telling what the end of it might be; what did he go for, that was what he wanted to know? He wished the young fellow no harm, but why did he go? Everybody echoed these words, and shook their heads again, having done which they wished John Podgers good night, and straggled home to bed.

The Kingston people were in their first sleep when Will Marks and his conductor rode through the town and up to the door of a house where sundry grave functionaries were assembled, anxiously expecting the arrival of the renowned Podgers. They were a little disappointed to find a gay young man in his place; but they put the best face upon the matter, and gave him full instructions how he was to conceal himself behind the gibbet, and watch and listen to the witches, and how at a certain time he was to burst forth and cut and slash among them vigorously, so that the suspected parties might be found bleeding in their beds next day, and thoroughly confounded. They gave him a great quantity of wholesome advice besides, and—which was more to the purpose with Will—a good supper. All these things being done, and midnight nearly come, they sallied forth to show him the spot where he was to keep his dreary vigil.

The night was by this time dark and threatening. There was a rumbling of distant thunder, and a low sighing of wind among the trees, which was very dismal. The potentates of the town kept so uncommonly close to Will that they trod upon his toes, or stumbled against his ankles, or nearly tripped up his heels at every step he took, and, besides these annoyances, their teeth chattered so with fear, that he seemed to be accompanied by a dirge of castanets.

At last they made a halt at the opening of a lonely, desolate space, and, pointing to a black object at some distance, asked Will if he saw that, yonder.

'Yes,' he replied. 'What then?'

Informing him abruptly that it was the gibbet where he was to watch, they wished him good night in an extremely friendly manner, and ran back as fast as their feet would carry them.

Will walked boldly to the gibbet, and, glancing upwards when he came under it, saw—certainly with satisfaction—that it was empty, and that nothing dangled from the top but some iron chains, which swung mournfully to and fro as they were moved by the breeze. After a careful survey of every quarter he determined to take his station with his face towards the town; both because that would place him with his back to the wind, and because, if any trick or surprise were attempted, it would probably come from that direction in the first instance. Having taken these precautions, he wrapped his cloak about him so that it left the handle of his sword free, and ready to his hand, and leaning against the gallows-tree with his cap not quite so much on one side as it had been before, took up his position for the night.

SECOND CHAPTER OF MR. PICKWICK'S TALE

We left Will Marks leaning under the gibbet with his face towards the town, scanning the distance with a keen eye, which sought to pierce the darkness and catch the earliest glimpse of any person or persons that might approach towards him. But all was quiet, and, save the howling of the wind as it swept across the heath in gusts, and the creaking of the chains that dangled above his head, there was no sound to break the sullen stillness of the night. After half an hour or so this monotony became more disconcerting to Will than the most furious uproar would have been, and he heartily wished for some one antagonist with whom he might have a fair stand-up fight, if it were only to warm himself.

Truth to tell, it was a bitter wind, and seemed to blow to the very heart of a man whose blood, heated but now with rapid riding, was the more sensitive to the chilling blast. Will was a daring fellow, and cared not a jot for hard knocks or sharp blades; but he could not persuade himself to move or walk about, having just that vague expectation of a sudden assault which made it a comfortable thing to have something at his back, even though that something were a gallows-tree. He had no great faith in the superstitions of the age, still such of them as occurred to him did not serve to lighten the time, or to render his situation the more endurable. He remembered how witches were said to repair at that ghostly hour to churchyards and gibbets, and such-like dismal spots, to pluck the bleeding mandrake or scrape the flesh from dead men's bones, as choice ingredients for their spells; how, stealing by night to lonely places, they dug graves with their finger-nails, or anointed themselves before riding in the air, with a delicate pomatum made of the fat of infants newly boiled. These, and many other fabled practices of a no less agreeable nature, and all having some reference to the circumstances in which he was placed, passed and repassed in quick succession through the mind of Will Marks, and adding a shadowy dread to that distrust and watchfulness which his situation inspired, rendered it, upon the whole, sufficiently uncomfortable. As he had foreseen, too, the rain began to descend heavily, and driving before the wind in a thick mist, obscured even those few objects which the darkness of the night had before imperfectly revealed.

'Look!' shrieked a voice. 'Great Heaven, it has fallen down, and stands erect as if it lived!'

The speaker was close behind him; the voice was almost at his ear. Will threw off his cloak, drew his sword, and darting swiftly round, seized a woman by the wrist, who, recoiling from him with a dreadful shriek, fell struggling upon her knees. Another woman, clad, like her whom he had grasped, in mourning garments, stood rooted to the spot on which they were, gazing upon his face with wild and glaring eyes that quite appalled him.

'Say,' cried Will, when they had confronted each other thus for some time, 'what are ye?'

'Say what are *you*,' returned the woman, 'who trouble even this obscene resting-place of the dead, and strip the gibbet of its honoured burden? Where is the body?'

He looked in wonder and affright from the woman who questioned him to the other whose arm he clutched.

'Where is the body?' repeated the questioner more firmly than before. 'You wear no livery which marks you for the hireling of the government. You are no friend to us, or I should recognise you, for the friends of such as we are few in number. What are you then, and wherefore are you here?'

'I am no foe to the distressed and helpless,' said Will. 'Are ye among that number? ye should be by your looks.'

'We are!' was the answer.

'Is it ye who have been wailing and weeping here under cover of the night?' said Will.

'It is,' replied the woman sternly; and pointing, as she spoke, towards her companion, 'she mourns a husband, and I a brother. Even the bloody law that wreaks its vengeance on the dead does not make that a crime, and if it did 'twould be alike to us who are past its fear or favour.'

Will glanced at the two females, and could barely discern that the one whom he addressed was much the elder, and that the other was young and of a slight figure. Both were deadly pale, their garments wet and worn, their hair dishevelled and streaming in the wind, themselves bowed down with grief and misery; their whole appearance most dejected, wretched, and forlorn. A sight so different from any he had expected to encounter touched him to the quick, and all idea of anything but their pitiable condition vanished before it.

'I am a rough, blunt yeoman,' said Will. 'Why I came here is told in a word; you have been overheard at a distance in the silence of the night, and I have undertaken a watch for hags or spirits. I came here expecting an adventure, and prepared to go through with any. If there be aught that I can do to help or aid you, name it, and on the faith of a man who can be secret and trusty, I will stand by you to the death.'

'How comes this gibbet to be empty?' asked the elder female.

'I swear to you,' replied Will, 'that I know as little as yourself. But this I know, that when I came here an hour ago or so, it was as it is now; and if, as I gather from your question, it was not so last night, sure I am that it has been secretly disturbed without the knowledge of the folks in yonder town. Bethink you, therefore, whether you have no friends in league with you or with him on whom the law has done its worst, by whom these sad remains have been removed for burial.'

The women spoke together, and Will retired a pace or two while they conversed apart. He could hear them sob and moan, and saw that they wrung their hands in fruitless agony. He could make out little that they said, but between whiles he gathered enough to assure him that his suggestion was not very wide of the mark, and that they not only suspected by whom the body had been removed, but also whither it had been conveyed. When they had been in conversation a long time, they turned towards him once more. This time the younger female spoke.

'You have offered us your help?'

'I have.'

'And given a pledge that you are still willing to redeem?'

'Yes. So far as I may, keeping all plots and conspiracies at arm's length.'

'Follow us, friend.'

Will, whose self-possession was now quite restored, needed no second bidding, but with his drawn sword in his hand, and his cloak so muffled over his left arm as to serve for a kind of shield without offering any impediment to its free action, suffered them to lead the way. Through mud and mire, and wind and rain, they walked in silence a full mile. At length they turned into a dark lane, where, suddenly starting out from beneath some trees where he had taken shelter, a man appeared, having in his charge three saddled horses. One of these (his own apparently), in obedience to a whisper from the women, he consigned to Will, who, seeing that they mounted, mounted also. Then, without a word spoken, they rode on together, leaving the attendant behind.

They made no halt nor slackened their pace until they arrived near Putney. At a large wooden house which stood apart from any other they alighted, and giving their horses to one who was already waiting, passed in by a side door, and so up some narrow creaking stairs into a small panelled chamber, where Will was left alone. He had not been here very long, when the door was softly opened, and there entered to him a cavalier whose face was concealed beneath a black mask.

Will stood upon his guard, and scrutinised this figure from head to foot. The form was that of a man pretty far advanced in life, but of a firm and stately carriage. His dress was of a rich and costly kind, but so soiled and disordered that it was scarcely to be recognised for one of those gorgeous suits which the expensive taste and fashion of the time prescribed for men of any rank or station.

He was booted and spurred, and bore about him even as many tokens of the state of the roads as Will himself. All this he noted, while the eyes behind the mask regarded him with equal attention. This survey over, the cavalier broke silence.

'Thou'rt young and bold, and wouldst be richer than thou art?'

'The two first I am,' returned Will. 'The last I have scarcely thought of. But be it so. Say that I would be richer than I am; what then?'

'The way lies before thee now,' replied the Mask.

'Show it me.'

'First let me inform thee, that thou wert brought here to-night lest thou shouldst too soon have told thy tale to those who placed thee on the watch.'

'I thought as much when I followed,' said Will. 'But I am no blab, not I.'

'Good,' returned the Mask. 'Now listen. He who was to have executed the enterprise of burying that body, which, as thou hast suspected, was taken down to-night, has left us in our need.'

Will nodded, and thought within himself that if the Mask were to attempt to play any tricks, the first eyelet-hole on the left-hand side of his doublet, counting from the buttons up the front, would be a very good place in which to pink him neatly.

'Thou art here, and the emergency is desperate. I propose his task to thee. Convey the body (now coffined in this house), by means that I shall show, to the Church of St. Dunstan in London to-morrow night, and thy service shall be richly paid. Thou'rt about to ask whose corpse it is. Seek not to know. I warn thee, seek not to know. Felons hang in chains on every moor and heath. Believe, as others do, that this was one, and ask no further. The murders of state policy, its victims or avengers, had best remain unknown to such as thee.'

'The mystery of this service,' said Will, 'bespeaks its danger. What is the reward?'

'One hundred golden unities,' replied the cavalier. 'The danger to one who cannot be recognised as the friend of a fallen cause is not great, but there is some hazard to be run. Decide between that and the reward.'

'What if I refuse?' said Will.

'Depart in peace, in God's name,' returned the Mask in a melancholy tone, 'and keep our secret, remembering that those who brought thee here were crushed and stricken women, and that those who bade thee go free could have had thy life with one word, and no man the wiser.'

Men were readier to undertake desperate adventures in those times than they are now. In this case the temptation was great, and the punishment, even in case of detection, was not likely to be very severe, as Will came of a loyal stock, and his uncle was in good repute, and a passable tale to account for his possession of the body and his ignorance of the identity might be easily devised.

The cavalier explained that a coveted cart had been prepared for the purpose; that the time of departure could be arranged so that he should reach London Bridge at dusk, and proceed through the City after the day had closed in; that people would be ready at his journey's end to place the coffin in a vault without a minute's delay; that officious inquirers in the streets would be easily repelled by the tale that he was carrying for interment the corpse of one who had died of the plague; and in short showed him every reason why he should succeed, and none why he should fail. After a time they were joined by another gentleman, masked like the first, who added new arguments to those which had been already urged; the wretched wife, too, added her tears and prayers to their calmer representations; and in the end, Will, moved by compassion and good-nature, by a love of the marvellous, by a mischievous anticipation of the terrors of the Kingston people when he should be missing next day, and finally, by the prospect of gain, took upon himself the task, and devoted all his energies to its successful execution.

The following night, when it was quite dark, the hollow echoes of old London Bridge responded to the rumbling of the cart which contained the ghastly load, the object of Will Marks' care. Sufficiently disguised to attract no attention by his garb, Will walked at the horse's head, as unconcerned as a man could be who was sensible that he had now arrived at the most dangerous part of his undertaking, but full of boldness and confidence.

It was now eight o'clock. After nine, none could walk the streets without danger of their lives, and even at this hour, robberies and murder were of no uncommon occurrence. The shops upon the bridge were all closed; the low wooden arches thrown across the way were like so many black pits, in every one of which ill-favoured fellows lurked in knots of three or four; some standing upright against the wall, lying in wait; others skulking in gateways, and thrusting out their uncombed heads and scowling eyes: others crossing and recrossing, and constantly jostling both horse and man to provoke a quarrel; others stealing away and summoning their companions in a low whistle. Once, even in that short passage, there was the noise of scuffling and the clash of swords behind him, but Will, who knew the City and its ways, kept straight on and scarcely turned his head.

The streets being unpaved, the rain of the night before had converted them into a perfect quagmire, which the splashing water- spouts from the gables, and the filth and offal cast from the different houses, swelled in no small degree. These odious matters being left to putrefy in the close and heavy air, emitted an insupportable stench, to which every court and passage poured forth a contribution of its own. Many parts, even of the main streets, with their projecting stories tottering overhead and nearly shutting out the sky, were more like huge chimneys than open ways. At the corners of some of these, great bonfires were burning to prevent infection from the plague, of which it was rumoured that some citizens had lately died; and few, who availing themselves of the light thus afforded paused for a moment to look around them, would have been disposed to doubt the existence of the disease, or wonder at its dreadful visitations.

But it was not in such scenes as these, or even in the deep and miry road, that Will Marks found the chief obstacles to his progress. There were kites and ravens feeding in the streets (the only scavengers the City kept), who, scenting what he carried, followed the cart or fluttered on its top, and croaked their knowledge of its burden and their ravenous appetite for prey. There were distant fires, where the poor wood and plaster tenements wasted fiercely, and whither crowds made their way, clamouring eagerly for plunder, beating down all who came within their reach, and yelling like devils let loose. There were single-handed men flying from bands of ruffians, who pursued them with naked weapons, and hunted them savagely; there were drunken, desperate robbers issuing from their dens and staggering through the open streets where no man dared molest them; there were vagabond servitors returning from the Bear Garden, where had been good sport that day, dragging after them their torn and bleeding dogs, or leaving them to die and rot upon the road. Nothing was abroad but cruelty, violence, and disorder.

Many were the interruptions which Will Marks encountered from these stragglers, and many the narrow escapes he made. Now some stout bully would take his seat upon the cart, insisting to be driven to his own home, and now two or three men would come down upon him together, and demand that on peril of his life he showed them what he had inside. Then a party of the city watch, upon their rounds, would draw across the road, and not satisfied with his tale, question him closely, and revenge themselves by a little cuffing and hustling for maltreatment sustained at other hands that night. All these assailants had to be rebutted, some by fair words, some by foul, and some by blows. But Will Marks was not the man to be stopped or turned back now he had penetrated so far, and though he got on slowly, still he made his way down Fleet-street and reached the church at last.

As he had been forewarned, all was in readiness. Directly he stopped, the coffin was removed by four men, who appeared so suddenly that they seemed to have started from the earth. A fifth mounted the cart, and scarcely allowing Will time to snatch from it a little bundle containing such of his own clothes as he had thrown off on assuming his disguise, drove briskly away. Will never saw cart or man again.

He followed the body into the church, and it was well he lost no time in doing so, for the door was immediately closed. There was no light in the building save that which came from a couple of torches borne by two men in cloaks, who stood upon the brink of a vault. Each supported a female figure, and all observed a profound silence.

By this dim and solemn glare, which made Will feel as though light itself were dead, and its tomb the dreary arches that frowned above, they placed the coffin in the vault, with uncovered heads, and closed it up. One of the torch-bearers then turned to Will, and stretched forth his hand, in which was a purse of gold. Something told him directly that those were the same eyes which he had seen beneath the mask.

'Take it,' said the cavalier in a low voice, 'and be happy. Though these have been hasty obsequies, and no priest has blessed the work, there will not be the less peace with thee thereafter, for having laid his bones beside those of his little children. Keep thy own counsel, for thy sake no less than ours, and God be with thee!'

'The blessing of a widowed mother on thy head, good friend!' cried the younger lady through her tears; 'the blessing of one who has now no hope or rest but in this grave!'

Will stood with the purse in his hand, and involuntarily made a gesture as though he would return it, for though a thoughtless fellow, he was of a frank and generous nature. But the two gentlemen, extinguishing their torches, cautioned him to be gone, as their common safety would be endangered by a longer delay; and at the same time their retreating footsteps sounded through the church. He turned, therefore, towards the point at which he had entered, and seeing by a faint gleam in the distance that the door was again partially open, groped his way towards it and so passed into the street.

Meantime the local authorities of Kingston had kept watch and ward all the previous night, fancying every now and then that dismal shrieks were borne towards them on the wind, and frequently winking to each other, and drawing closer to the fire as they drank the health of the lonely sentinel, upon whom a clerical gentleman present was especially severe by reason of his levity and youthful folly. Two or three of the gravest in company, who were of a theological turn, propounded to him the question, whether such a character was not but poorly armed for single combat with the Devil, and whether he himself would not have been a stronger opponent; but the clerical gentleman, sharply reproving them for their presumption in discussing such questions, clearly showed that a fitter champion than Will could scarcely have been selected, not only for that being a child of Satan, he was the less likely to be alarmed by the appearance of his own father, but because Satan himself would be at his ease in such company, and would not scruple to kick up his heels to an extent which it was quite certain he would never venture before clerical eyes, under whose influence (as was notorious) he became quite a tame and milk-and-water character.

But when next morning arrived, and with it no Will Marks, and when a strong party repairing to the spot, as a strong party ventured to do in broad day, found Will gone and the gibbet empty, matters grew serious indeed. The day passing away and no news arriving, and the night going on also without any intelligence, the thing grew more tremendous still; in short, the neighbourhood worked itself up to such a comfortable pitch of mystery and horror, that it is a great question whether the general feeling was not one of excessive disappointment, when, on the second morning, Will Marks returned.

However this may be, back Will came in a very cool and collected state, and appearing not to trouble himself much about anybody except old John Podgers, who, having been sent for, was sitting in the Town Hall crying slowly, and dozing between whiles. Having embraced his uncle and assured him of his safety, Will mounted on a table and told his story to the crowd.

And surely they would have been the most unreasonable crowd that ever assembled together, if they had been in the least respect disappointed with the tale he told them; for besides describing the Witches' Dance to the minutest motion of their legs, and performing it in character on the table, with the assistance of a broomstick, he related how they had carried off the body in a copper caldron, and so bewitched him, that he lost his senses until he found himself lying under a hedge at least ten miles off, whence he had straightway returned as they then beheld. The story gained such universal applause that it soon afterwards brought down express from London the great witch-finder of the age, the Heaven-born Hopkins, who having examined Will closely on several points, pronounced it the most extraordinary and the best accredited witch- story ever known, under which title it was published at the Three Bibles on London Bridge, in small quarto, with a view of the caldron from an original drawing, and a portrait of the clerical gentleman as he sat by the fire.

On one point Will was particularly careful: and that was to describe for the witches he had seen, three impossible old females, whose likenesses never were or will be. Thus he saved the lives of the suspected parties, and of all other old women who were dragged before him to be identified.

This circumstance occasioned John Podgers much grief and sorrow, until happening one day to cast his eyes upon his house-keeper, and observing her to be plainly afflicted with rheumatism, he procured her to be burnt as an undoubted witch. For this service to the state he was immediately knighted, and became from that time Sir John Podgers.

Will Marks never gained any clue to the mystery in which he had been an actor, nor did any inscription in the church, which he often visited afterwards, nor any of the limited inquiries that he dared to make, yield him the least assistance. As he kept his own secret, he was compelled to spend the gold discreetly and sparingly. In the course of time he married the young lady of whom I have already told you, whose maiden name is not recorded, with whom he led a prosperous and happy life. Years and years after this adventure, it was his wont to tell her upon a stormy night that it was a great comfort to him to think those bones, to whomsoever they might have once belonged, were not bleaching in the troubled air, but were mouldering away with the dust of their own kith and kindred in a quiet grave.

FURTHER PARTICULARS OF MASTER HUMPHREY'S VISITOR

Being very full of Mr. Pickwick's application, and highly pleased with the compliment he had paid me, it will be readily supposed that long before our next night of meeting I communicated it to my three friends, who unanimously voted his admission into our body. We all looked forward with some impatience to the occasion which would enroll him among us, but I am greatly mistaken if Jack Redburn and myself were not by many degrees the most impatient of the party.

At length the night came, and a few minutes after ten Mr. Pickwick's knock was heard at the street-door. He was shown into a lower room, and I directly took my crooked stick and went to accompany him up-stairs, in order that he might be presented with all honour and formality.

'Mr. Pickwick,' said I, on entering the room, 'I am rejoiced to see you,—rejoiced to believe that this is but the opening of a long series of visits to this house, and but the beginning of a close and lasting friendship.'

That gentleman made a suitable reply with a cordiality and frankness peculiarly his own, and glanced with a smile towards two persons behind the door, whom I had not at first observed, and whom I immediately recognised as Mr. Samuel Weller and his father.

It was a warm evening, but the elder Mr. Weller was attired, notwithstanding, in a most capacious greatcoat, and his chin enveloped in a large speckled shawl, such as is usually worn by stage coachmen on active service. He looked very rosy and very stout, especially about the legs, which appeared to have been compressed into his top-boots with some difficulty. His broad- brimmed hat he held under his left arm, and with the forefinger of his right hand he touched his forehead a great many times in acknowledgment of my presence.

'I am very glad to see you in such good health, Mr. Weller,' said I.

'Why, thankee, sir,' returned Mr. Weller, 'the axle an't broke yet. We keeps up a steady pace,—not too sewere, but vith a moderate degree o' friction,—and the consekens is that ve're still a runnin' and comes in to the time reg'lar.—My son Samivel, sir, as you may have read on in history,' added Mr. Weller, introducing his first-born.

I received Sam very graciously, but before he could say a word his father struck in again.

'Samivel Veller, sir,' said the old gentleman, 'has conferred upon me the ancient title o' grandfather vich had long laid dormouse, and wos s'posed to be nearly hex-tinct in our family. Sammy, relate a anecdote o' vun o' them boys,—that 'ere little anecdote about young Tony sayin' as he *would* smoke a pipe unbeknown to his mother.'

'Be quiet, can't you?' said Sam; 'I never see such a old magpie—never!'

'That 'ere Tony is the blessedest boy,' said Mr. Weller, heedless of this rebuff, 'the blessedest boy as ever I see in *my* days! of all the charmin'est infants as ever I heerd tell on, includin' them as was kivered over by the robin-redbreasts arter they'd committed sooicide with blackberries, there never wos any like that 'ere little Tony. He's alvays a playin' vith a quart pot, that boy is! To see him a settin' down on the doorstep pretending to drink out of it, and fetching a long breath artervards, and smoking a bit of firevood, and sayin', "Now I'm grandfather,"—to see him a doin' that at two year old is better than any play as wos ever wrote. "Now I'm grandfather!" He wouldn't take a pint pot if you wos to make him a present on it, but he gets his quart, and then he says, "Now I'm grandfather!"'

Mr. Weller was so overpowered by this picture that he straightway fell into a most alarming fit of coughing, which must certainly have been attended with some fatal result but for the dexterity and promptitude of Sam, who, taking a firm grasp of the shawl just under his father's chin, shook him to and fro with great violence, at the same time administering some smart blows between his shoulders. By this curious mode of treatment Mr. Weller was finally recovered, but with a very crimson face, and in a state of great exhaustion.

'He'll do now, Sam,' said Mr. Pickwick, who had been in some alarm himself.

'He'll do, sir!' cried Sam, looking reproachfully at his parent. 'Yes, he *will* do one o' these days,—he'll do for his-self and then he'll wish he hadn't. Did anybody ever see sich a inconsiderate old file,—laughing into conwulsions afore company, and stamping on the floor as if he'd brought his own carpet vith him and wos under a wager to punch the pattern out in a given time? He'll begin again in a minute. There—he's a goin' off—I said he would!'

In fact, Mr. Weller, whose mind was still running upon his precocious grandson, was seen to shake his head from side to side, while a laugh, working like an earthquake, below the surface, produced various extraordinary appearances in his face, chest, and shoulders,—the more alarming because unaccompanied by any noise whatever. These emotions, however, gradually subsided, and after three or four short relapses he wiped his eyes with the cuff of his coat, and looked about him with tolerable composure.

'Afore the governor vith-draws,' said Mr. Weller, 'there is a pint, respecting vich Sammy has a qvestion to ask. Vile that qvestion is a perwadin' this here conwersation, p'raps the genl'men vill permit me to re-tire.'

'Wot are you goin' away for?' demanded Sam, seizing his father by the coat-tail.

'I never see such a undootiful boy as you, Samivel,' returned Mr. Weller. 'Didn't you make a solemn promise, amountin' almost to a speeches o' wow, that you'd put that 'ere qvestion on my account?'

'Well, I'm agreeable to do it,' said Sam, 'but not if you go cuttin' away like that, as the bull turned round and mildly observed to the drover ven they wos a goadin' him into the butcher's door. The fact is, sir,' said Sam, addressing me, 'that he wants to know somethin' respectin' that 'ere lady as is housekeeper here.'

'Ay. What is that?'

'Vy, sir,' said Sam, grinning still more, 'he wishes to know vether she—'

'In short,' interposed old Mr. Weller decisively, a perspiration breaking out upon his forehead, 'vether that 'ere old creetur is or is not a widder.'

Mr. Pickwick laughed heartily, and so did I, as I replied decisively, that 'my housekeeper was a spinster.'

'There!' cried Sam, 'now you're satisfied. You hear she's a spinster.'

'A wot?' said his father, with deep scorn.

'A spinster,' replied Sam.

Mr. Weller looked very hard at his son for a minute or two, and then said,

'Never mind vether she makes jokes or not, that's no matter. Wot I say is, is that 'ere female a widder, or is she not?'

'Wot do you mean by her making jokes?' demanded Sam, quite aghast at the obscurity of his parent's speech.

'Never you mind, Samivel,' returned Mr. Weller gravely; 'puns may be wery good things or they may be wery bad 'uns, and a female may be none the better or she may be none the vurse for making of 'em; that's got nothing to do vith widders.'

'Wy now,' said Sam, looking round, 'would anybody believe as a man at his time o' life could be running his head agin spinsters and punsters being the same thing?'

'There an't a straw's difference between 'em,' said Mr. Weller. 'Your father didn't drive a coach for so many years, not to be ekal to his own langvidge as far as *that* goes, Sammy.'

Avoiding the question of etymology, upon which the old gentleman's mind was quite made up, he was several times assured that the housekeeper had never been married. He expressed great satisfaction on hearing this, and apologised for the question, remarking that he had been greatly terrified by a widow not long before, and that his natural timidity was increased in consequence.

'It wos on the rail,' said Mr. Weller, with strong emphasis; 'I wos a goin' down to Birmingham by the rail, and I wos locked up in a close carriage vith a living widder. Alone we wos; the widder and me wos alone; and I believe it wos only because we WOS alone and there wos no clergyman in the conwayance, that that 'ere widder didn't marry me afore ve reached the half-way station. Ven I think how she began a screaming as we wos a goin' under them tunnels in the dark,—how she kept on a faintin' and ketchin' hold o' me,—and how I tried to bust open the door as was tight-locked and perwented all escape—Ah! It was a awful thing, most awful!'

Mr. Weller was so very much overcome by this retrospect that he was unable, until he had wiped his brow several times, to return any reply to the question whether he approved of railway communication, notwithstanding that it would appear from the answer which he ultimately gave, that he entertained strong opinions on the subject.

'I con-sider,' said Mr. Weller, 'that the rail is unconstitootional and an inwaser o' priwileges, and I should wery much like to know what that 'ere old Carter as once stood up for our liberties and wun 'em too,—I should like to know wot he vould say, if he wos alive now, to Englishmen being locked up vith widders, or with anybody again their wills. Wot a old Carter would have said, a old Coachman may say, and I as-sert that in that pint o' view alone, the rail is an inwaser. As to the comfort, vere's the comfort o' sittin' in a harm-cheer lookin' at brick walls or heaps o' mud, never comin' to a public-house, never seein' a glass o' ale, never goin' through a pike, never meetin' a change o' no kind (horses or othervise), but alvays comin' to a place, ven you come to one at all, the wery picter o' the last, vith the same p'leesemen standing about, the same blessed old bell a ringin', the same unfort'nate people standing behind the bars, a waitin' to be let in; and everythin' the same except the name, vich is wrote up in the same sized letters as the last name, and vith the same colours. As to the Honour and dignity o' travellin', vere can that be vithout a coachman; and wot's the rail to sich coachmen and guards as is sometimes forced to go by it, but a outrage and a insult? As to the pace, wot sort o' pace do you think I, Tony Veller, could have kept a coach goin' at, for five hundred thousand pound a mile, paid in adwance afore the coach was on the road? And as to the ingein,—a nasty, wheezin', creakin', gaspin', puffin', bustin' monster, alvays out o' breath, vith a shiny green-and-gold back, like a unpleasant beetle in that 'ere gas magnifier,—as to the ingein as is alvays a pourin' out red-hot coals at night, and black smoke in the day, the sensiblest thing it does, in my opinion, is, ven there's somethin' in the vay, and it sets up that 'ere frightful scream vich seems to say, "Now here's two hundred and forty passengers in the wery greatest extremity o' danger, and here's their two hundred and forty screams in vun!"'

By this time I began to fear that my friends would be rendered impatient by my protracted absence. I therefore begged Mr. Pickwick to accompany me up-stairs, and left the two Mr. Wellers in the care of the housekeeper, laying strict injunctions upon her to treat them with all possible hospitality.

CHAPTER IV—THE CLOCK

As we were going up-stairs, Mr. Pickwick put on his spectacles, which he had held in his hand hitherto; arranged his neckerchief, smoothed down his waistcoat, and made many other little preparations of that kind which men are accustomed to be mindful of, when they are going among strangers for the first time, and are anxious to impress them pleasantly. Seeing that I smiled, he smiled too, and said that if it had occurred to him before he left home, he would certainly have presented himself in pumps and silk stockings.

'I would, indeed, my dear sir,' he said very seriously; 'I would have shown my respect for the society, by laying aside my gaiters.'

'You may rest assured,' said I, 'that they would have regretted your doing so very much, for they are quite attached to them.'

'No, really!' cried Mr. Pickwick, with manifest pleasure. 'Do you think they care about my gaiters? Do you seriously think that they identify me at all with my gaiters?'

'I am sure they do,' I replied.

'Well, now,' said Mr. Pickwick, 'that is one of the most charming and agreeable circumstances that could possibly have occurred to me!'

I should not have written down this short conversation, but that it developed a slight point in Mr. Pickwick's character, with which I was not previously acquainted. He has a secret pride in his legs. The manner in which he spoke, and the accompanying glance he bestowed upon his tights, convince me that Mr. Pickwick regards his legs with much innocent vanity.

'But here are our friends,' said I, opening the door and taking his arm in mine; 'let them speak for themselves.—Gentlemen, I present to you Mr. Pickwick.'

Mr. Pickwick and I must have been a good contrast just then. I, leaning quietly on my crutch-stick, with something of a care-worn, patient air; he, having hold of my arm, and bowing in every direction with the most elastic politeness, and an expression of face whose sprightly cheerfulness and good-humour knew no bounds. The difference between us must have been more striking yet, as we advanced towards the table, and the amiable gentleman, adapting his jocund step to my poor tread, had his attention divided between treating my infirmities with the utmost consideration, and affecting to be wholly unconscious that I required any.

I made him personally known to each of my friends in turn. First, to the deaf gentleman, whom he regarded with much interest, and accosted with great frankness and cordiality. He had evidently some vague idea, at the moment, that my friend being deaf must be dumb also; for when the latter opened his lips to express the pleasure it afforded him to know a gentleman of whom he had heard so much, Mr. Pickwick was so extremely disconcerted, that I was obliged to step in to his relief.

His meeting with Jack Redburn was quite a treat to see. Mr. Pickwick smiled, and shook hands, and looked at him through his spectacles, and under them, and over them, and nodded his head approvingly, and then nodded to me, as much as to say, 'This is just the man; you were quite right;' and then turned to Jack and said a few hearty words, and then did and said everything over again with unimpaired vivacity. As to Jack himself, he was quite as much delighted with Mr. Pickwick as Mr. Pickwick could possibly be with him. Two people never can have met together since the world began, who exchanged a warmer or more enthusiastic greeting.

It was amusing to observe the difference between this encounter and that which succeeded, between Mr. Pickwick and Mr. Miles. It was clear that the latter gentleman viewed our new member as a kind of rival in the affections of Jack Redburn, and besides this, he had more than once hinted to me, in secret, that although he had no doubt Mr. Pickwick was a very worthy man, still he did consider that some of his exploits were unbecoming a gentleman of his years and gravity. Over and above these grounds of distrust, it is one of his fixed opinions, that the law never can by possibility do anything wrong; he therefore looks upon Mr. Pickwick as one who has justly suffered in purse and peace for a breach of his plighted faith to an unprotected female, and holds that he is called upon to regard him with some suspicion on that account. These causes led to a rather cold and formal reception; which Mr. Pickwick acknowledged with the same stateliness and intense politeness as was displayed on the other side. Indeed, he assumed an air of such majestic defiance, that I was fearful he might break out into some solemn protest or declaration, and therefore inducted him into his chair without a moment's delay.

This piece of generalship was perfectly successful. The instant he took his seat, Mr. Pickwick surveyed us all with a most benevolent aspect, and was taken with a fit of smiling full five minutes long. His interest in our ceremonies was immense. They are not very numerous or complicated, and a description of them may be comprised in very few words. As our transactions have already been, and must necessarily continue to be, more or less anticipated by being presented in these pages at different times, and under various forms, they do not require a detailed account.

Our first proceeding when we are assembled is to shake hands all round, and greet each other with cheerful and pleasant looks. Remembering that we assemble not only for the promotion of our happiness, but with the view of adding something to the common stock, an air of languor or indifference in any member of our body would be regarded by the others as a kind of treason. We have never had an offender in this respect; but if we had, there is no doubt that he would be taken to task pretty severely.

Our salutation over, the venerable piece of antiquity from which we take our name is wound up in silence. The ceremony is always performed by Master Humphrey himself (in treating of the club, I may be permitted to assume the historical style, and speak of myself in the third person), who mounts upon a chair for the purpose, armed with a large key. While it is in progress, Jack Redburn is required to keep at the farther end of the room under the guardianship of Mr. Miles, for he is known to entertain certain aspiring and unhallowed thoughts connected with the clock, and has even gone so far as to state that if he might take the works out for a day or two, he thinks he could improve them. We pardon him his presumption in consideration of his good intentions, and his keeping this respectful distance, which last penalty is insisted on, lest by secretly wounding the object of our regard in some tender part, in the ardour of his zeal for its improvement, he should fill us with dismay and consternation.

This regulation afforded Mr. Pickwick the highest delight, and seemed, if possible, to exalt Jack in his good opinion.

The next ceremony is the opening of the clock-case (of which Master Humphrey has likewise the key), the taking from it as many papers as will furnish forth our evening's entertainment, and arranging in the recess such new contributions as have been provided since our last meeting. This is always done with peculiar solemnity. The deaf gentleman then fills and lights his pipe, and we once more take our seats round the table before mentioned, Master Humphrey acting as president,—if we can be said to have any president, where all are on the same social footing,—and our friend Jack as secretary. Our preliminaries being now concluded, we fall into any train of conversation that happens to suggest itself, or proceed immediately to one of our readings. In the latter case, the paper selected is consigned to Master Humphrey, who flattens it carefully on the table and makes dog's ears in the corner of every page, ready for turning over easily; Jack Redburn trims the lamp with a small machine of his own invention which usually puts it out; Mr. Miles looks on with great approval notwithstanding; the deaf gentleman draws in his chair, so that he can follow the words on the paper or on Master Humphrey's lips as he pleases;

and Master Humphrey himself, looking round with mighty gratification, and glancing up at his old clock, begins to read aloud.

Mr. Pickwick's face, while his tale was being read, would have attracted the attention of the dullest man alive. The complacent motion of his head and forefinger as he gently beat time, and corrected the air with imaginary punctuation, the smile that mantled on his features at every jocose passage, and the sly look he stole around to observe its effect, the calm manner in which he shut his eyes and listened when there was some little piece of description, the changing expression with which he acted the dialogue to himself, his agony that the deaf gentleman should know what it was all about, and his extraordinary anxiety to correct the reader when he hesitated at a word in the manuscript, or substituted a wrong one, were alike worthy of remark. And when at last, endeavouring to communicate with the deaf gentleman by means of the finger alphabet, with which he constructed such words as are unknown in any civilised or savage language, he took up a slate and wrote in large text, one word in a line, the question, 'How—do—you—like—it?'—when he did this, and handing it over the table awaited the reply, with a countenance only brightened and improved by his great excitement, even Mr. Miles relaxed, and could not forbear looking at him for the moment with interest and favour.

'It has occurred to me,' said the deaf gentleman, who had watched Mr. Pickwick and everybody else with silent satisfaction—'it has occurred to me,' said the deaf gentleman, taking his pipe from his lips, 'that now is our time for filling our only empty chair.'

As our conversation had naturally turned upon the vacant seat, we lent a willing ear to this remark, and looked at our friend inquiringly.

'I feel sure,' said he, 'that Mr. Pickwick must be acquainted with somebody who would be an acquisition to us; that he must know the man we want. Pray let us not lose any time, but set this question at rest. Is it so, Mr. Pickwick?'

The gentleman addressed was about to return a verbal reply, but remembering our friend's infirmity, he substituted for this kind of answer some fifty nods. Then taking up the slate and printing on it a gigantic 'Yes,' he handed it across the table, and rubbing his hands as he looked round upon our faces, protested that he and the deaf gentleman quite understood each other, already.

'The person I have in my mind,' said Mr. Pickwick, 'and whom I should not have presumed to mention to you until some time hence, but for the opportunity you have given me, is a very strange old man. His name is Bamber.'

'Bamber!' said Jack. 'I have certainly heard the name before.'

'I have no doubt, then,' returned Mr. Pickwick, 'that you remember him in those adventures of mine (the Posthumous Papers of our old club, I mean), although he is only incidentally mentioned; and, if I remember right, appears but once.'

'That's it,' said Jack. 'Let me see. He is the person who has a grave interest in old mouldy chambers and the Inns of Court, and who relates some anecdotes having reference to his favourite theme,—and an odd ghost story,—is that the man?'

'The very same. Now,' said Mr. Pickwick, lowering his voice to a mysterious and confidential tone, 'he is a very extraordinary and remarkable person; living, and talking, and looking, like some strange spirit, whose delight is to haunt old buildings; and absorbed in that one subject which you have just mentioned, to an extent which is quite wonderful. When I retired into private life, I sought him out, and I do assure you that the more I see of him, the more strongly I am impressed with the strange and dreamy character of his mind.'

'Where does he live?' I inquired.

'He lives,' said Mr. Pickwick, 'in one of those dull, lonely old places with which his thoughts and stories are all connected; quite alone, and often shut up close for several weeks together. In this dusty solitude he broods upon the fancies he has so long indulged, and when he goes into the world, or anybody from the world without goes to see him, they are still present to his mind and still his favourite topic. I may say, I believe, that he has brought himself to entertain a regard for me, and an interest in my visits; feelings which I am certain he would extend to Master Humphrey's Clock if he were once tempted to join us. All I wish you to understand is, that he is a strange, secluded visionary, in the world but not of it; and as unlike anybody here as he is unlike anybody elsewhere that I have ever met or known.'

Mr. Miles received this account of our proposed companion with rather a wry face, and after murmuring that perhaps he was a little mad, inquired if he were rich.

'I never asked him,' said Mr. Pickwick.

'You might know, sir, for all that,' retorted Mr. Miles, sharply.

'Perhaps so, sir,' said Mr. Pickwick, no less sharply than the other, 'but I do not. Indeed,' he added, relapsing into his usual mildness, 'I have no means of judging. He lives poorly, but that would seem to be in keeping with his character. I never heard him allude to his circumstances, and never fell into the society of any man who had the slightest acquaintance with them. I have really told you all I know about him, and it rests with you to say whether you wish to know more, or know quite enough already.'

We were unanimously of opinion that we would seek to know more; and as a sort of compromise with Mr. Miles (who, although he said 'Yes—O certainly—he should like to know more about the gentleman—he had no right to put himself in opposition to the general wish,' and so forth, shook his head doubtfully and hemmed several times with peculiar gravity), it was arranged that Mr. Pickwick should carry me with him on an evening visit to the subject of our discussion, for which purpose an early appointment between that gentleman and myself was immediately agreed upon; it being understood that I was to act upon my own responsibility, and to invite him to join us or not, as I might think proper. This solemn question determined, we returned to the clock-case (where we have been forestalled by the reader), and between its contents, and the conversation they occasioned, the remainder of our time passed very quickly.

When we broke up, Mr. Pickwick took me aside to tell me that he had spent a most charming and delightful evening. Having made this communication with an air of the strictest secrecy, he took Jack Redburn into another corner to tell him the same, and then retired into another corner with the deaf gentleman and the slate, to repeat the assurance. It was amusing to observe the contest in his mind whether he should extend his confidence to Mr. Miles, or treat him with dignified reserve. Half a dozen times he stepped up behind him with a friendly air, and as often stepped back again without saying a word; at last, when he was close at that gentleman's ear and upon the very point of whispering something conciliating and agreeable, Mr. Miles happened suddenly to turn his head, upon which Mr. Pickwick skipped away, and said with some fierceness, 'Good night, sir—I was about to say good night, sir,—nothing more;' and so made a bow and left him.

'Now, Sam,' said Mr. Pickwick, when he had got down-stairs.

'All right, sir,' replied Mr. Weller. 'Hold hard, sir. Right arm fust—now the left—now one strong conwulsion, and the great- coat's on, sir.'

Mr. Pickwick acted upon these directions, and being further assisted by Sam, who pulled at one side of the collar, and Mr. Weller, who pulled hard at the other, was speedily enrobed. Mr. Weller, senior, then produced a full-sized stable lantern, which he had carefully deposited in a remote corner, on his arrival, and inquired whether Mr. Pickwick would have 'the lamps alight.'

'I think not to-night,' said Mr. Pickwick.

'Then if this here lady vill per-mit,' rejoined Mr. Weller, 'we'll leave it here, ready for next journey. This here lantern, mum,' said Mr. Weller, handing it to the housekeeper, 'vunce belonged to the celebrated Bill Blinder as is now at grass, as all on us vill be in our turns. Bill, mum, wos the hostler as had charge o' them two vell-known piebald leaders that run in the Bristol fast coach, and vould never go to no other tune but a sutherly vind and a cloudy sky, which wos consekvently played incessant, by the guard, wenever they wos on duty. He wos took wery bad one arternoon, arter having been off his feed, and wery shaky on his legs for some veeks; and he says to his mate, "Matey," he says, "I think I'm a- goin' the wrong side o' the post, and that my foot's wery near the bucket. Don't say I an't," he says, "for I know I am, and don't let me be interrupted," he says, "for I've saved a little money, and I'm a-goin' into the stable to make my last vill and testymint." "I'll take care as nobody interrupts," says his mate, "but you on'y hold up your head, and shake your ears a bit, and you're good for twenty years to come." Bill Blinder makes him no answer, but he goes avay into the stable, and there he soon artervards lays himself down a'tween the two piebalds, and dies,—previously a writin' outside the corn-chest, "This is the last vill and testymint of Villiam Blinder." They wos nat'rally wery much amazed at this, and arter looking among the litter, and up in the loft, and vere not, they opens the corn-chest, and finds that he'd been and chalked his vill inside the lid; so the lid was obligated to be took off the hinges, and sent up to Doctor Commons to be proved, and under that 'ere wery instrument this here lantern was passed to Tony Veller; vich circumstarnce, mum, gives it a wally in my eyes, and makes me rekvest, if you vill be so kind, as to take partickler care on it.'

The housekeeper graciously promised to keep the object of Mr. Weller's regard in the safest possible custody, and Mr. Pickwick, with a laughing face, took his leave. The bodyguard followed, side by side; old Mr. Weller buttoned and wrapped up from his boots to his chin; and Sam with his hands in his pockets and his hat half off his head, remonstrating with his father, as he went, on his extreme loquacity.

I was not a little surprised, on turning to go up-stairs, to encounter the barber in the passage at that late hour; for his attendance is usually confined to some half-hour in the morning. But Jack Redburn, who finds out (by instinct, I think) everything that happens in the house, informed me with great glee, that a society in imitation of our own had been that night formed in the kitchen, under the title of 'Mr. Weller's Watch,' of which the barber was a member; and that he could pledge himself to find means of making me acquainted with the whole of its future proceedings, which I begged him, both on my own account and that of my readers, by no means to neglect doing.

CHAPTER V—MR. WELLER'S WATCH

IT SEEMS that the housekeeper and the two Mr. Wellers were no sooner left together on the occasion of their first becoming acquainted, than the housekeeper called to her assistance Mr. Slithers the barber, who had been lurking in the kitchen in expectation of her summons; and with many smiles and much sweetness introduced him as one who would assist her in the responsible office of entertaining her distinguished visitors.

'Indeed,' said she, 'without Mr. Slithers I should have been placed in quite an awkward situation.'

'There is no call for any hock'erdness, mum,' said Mr. Weller with the utmost politeness; 'no call wotsumever. A lady,' added the old gentleman, looking about him with the air of one who establishes an incontrovertible position,—'a lady can't be hock'erd. Natur' has otherwise purwided.'

The housekeeper inclined her head and smiled yet more sweetly. The barber, who had been fluttering about Mr. Weller and Sam in a state of great anxiety to improve their acquaintance, rubbed his hands and cried, 'Hear, hear! Very true, sir;' whereupon Sam turned about and steadily regarded him for some seconds in silence.

'I never knew,' said Sam, fixing his eyes in a ruminative manner upon the blushing barber,—'I never knew but vun o' your trade, but *he* wos worth a dozen, and wos indeed dewoted to his callin'!'

'Was he in the easy shaving way, sir,' inquired Mr. Slithers; 'or in the cutting and curling line?'

'Both,' replied Sam; 'easy shavin' was his natur', and cuttin' and curlin' was his pride and glory. His whole delight wos in his trade. He spent all his money in bears, and run in debt for 'em besides, and there they wos a growling avay down in the front cellar all day long, and ineffectooally gnashing their teeth, vile the grease o' their relations and friends wos being re-tailed in gallipots in the shop above, and the first-floor winder wos ornamented vith their heads; not to speak o' the dreadful aggrawation it must have been to 'em to see a man alvays a walkin' up and down the pavement outside, vith the portrait of a bear in his last agonies, and underneath in large letters, "Another fine animal wos slaughtered yesterday at Jinkinson's!" Hows'ever, there they wos, and there Jinkinson wos, till he wos took wery ill with some inn'ard disorder, lost the use of his legs, and wos confined to his bed, vere he laid a wery long time, but sich wos his pride in his profession, even then, that wenever he wos worse than usual the doctor used to go down-stairs and say, "Jinkinson's wery low this mornin'; we must give the bears a stir;" and as sure as ever they stirred 'em up a bit and made 'em roar, Jinkinson opens his eyes if he wos ever so bad, calls out, "There's the bears!" and rewives agin.'

'Astonishing!' cried the barber.

'Not a bit,' said Sam, 'human natur' neat as imported. Vun day the doctor happenin' to say, "I shall look in as usual to-morrow mornin'," Jinkinson catches hold of his hand and says, "Doctor," he says, "will you grant me one favour?" "I will, Jinkinson," says the doctor. "Then, doctor," says Jinkinson, "vill you come unshaved, and let me shave you?" "I will," says the doctor. "God bless you," says Jinkinson. Next day the doctor came, and arter he'd been shaved all skilful and reg'lar, he says, "Jinkinson," he says, "it's wery plain this does you good. Now," he says, "I've got a coachman as has got a beard that it 'ud warm your heart to work on, and though the footman," he says, "hasn't got much of a beard, still he's a trying it on vith a pair o' viskers to that extent that razors is Christian charity. If they take it in turns to mind the carriage when it's a waitin' below," he says, "wot's to hinder you from operatin' on both of 'em ev'ry day as well as upon me? you've got six children," he says, "wot's to hinder you from shavin' all their heads and keepin' 'em shaved? you've got two assistants in the shop down-stairs, wot's to hinder you from cuttin' and curlin' them as often as you like? Do this," he says, "and you're a man agin." Jinkinson squeedged the doctor's hand and begun that wery day; he kept his tools upon the bed, and wenever he felt his-self gettin' worse, he turned to at vun o' the children who wos a runnin' about the house vith heads like clean Dutch cheeses, and shaved him agin. Vun day the lawyer come to make his vill; all the time he wos a takin' it down, Jinkinson was secretly a clippin' avay at his hair vith a large pair of scissors. "Wot's that 'ere snippin' noise?" says the lawyer every now and then; "it's like a man havin' his hair cut." "It *is* wery like a man havin' his hair cut," says poor Jinkinson, hidin' the scissors, and lookin' quite innocent. By the time the lawyer found it out, he was wery nearly bald. Jinkinson wos kept alive in this vay for a long time, but at last vun day he has in all the children vun arter another, shaves each on 'em wery clean, and gives him vun kiss on the crown o' his head; then he has in the two assistants, and arter cuttin' and curlin' of 'em in the first style of elegance, says he should like to hear the woice o' the greasiest bear, vich rekvest is immediately complied with; then he says that he feels wery happy in his mind and vishes to be left alone; and then he dies, previously cuttin' his own hair and makin' one flat curl in the wery middle of his forehead.'

This anecdote produced an extraordinary effect, not only upon Mr. Slithers, but upon the housekeeper also, who evinced so much anxiety to please and be pleased, that Mr. Weller, with a manner betokening some alarm, conveyed a whispered inquiry to his son whether he had gone 'too fur.'

'Wot do you mean by too fur?' demanded Sam.

'In that 'ere little compliment respectin' the want of hock'erdness in ladies, Sammy,' replied his father.

'You don't think she's fallen in love with you in consekens o' that, do you?' said Sam.

'More unlikelier things have come to pass, my boy,' replied Mr. Weller in a hoarse whisper; 'I'm always afeerd of inadwertent captiwation, Sammy. If I know'd how to make myself ugly or unpleasant, I'd do it, Samivel, rayther than live in this here state of perpetival terror!'

Mr. Weller had, at that time, no further opportunity of dwelling upon the apprehensions which beset his mind, for the immediate occasion of his fears proceeded to lead the way down-stairs, apologising as they went for conducting him into the kitchen, which apartment, however, she was induced to proffer for his accommodation in preference to her own little room, the rather as it afforded greater facilities for smoking, and was immediately adjoining the ale-cellar. The preparations which were already made sufficiently proved that these were not mere words of course, for on the deal table were a sturdy ale-jug and glasses, flanked with clean pipes and a plentiful supply of tobacco for the old gentleman and his son, while on a dresser hard by was goodly store of cold meat and other eatables. At sight of these arrangements Mr. Weller was at first distracted between his love of joviality and his doubts whether they were not to be considered as so many evidences of captivation having already taken place; but he soon yielded to his natural impulse, and took his seat at the table with a very jolly countenance.

'As to imbibin' any o' this here flagrant veed, mum, in the presence of a lady,' said Mr. Weller, taking up a pipe and laying it down again, 'it couldn't be. Samivel, total abstinence, if *you* please.'

'But I like it of all things,' said the housekeeper.

'No,' rejoined Mr. Weller, shaking his head,—'no.'

'Upon my word I do,' said the housekeeper. 'Mr. Slithers knows I do.'

Mr. Weller coughed, and notwithstanding the barber's confirmation of the statement, said 'No' again, but more feebly than before. The housekeeper lighted a piece of paper, and insisted on applying it to the bowl of the pipe with her own fair hands; Mr. Weller resisted; the housekeeper cried that her fingers would be burnt; Mr. Weller gave way. The pipe was ignited, Mr. Weller drew a long puff of smoke, and detecting himself in the very act of smiling on the housekeeper, put a sudden constraint upon his countenance and looked sternly at the candle, with a determination not to captivate, himself, or encourage thoughts of captivation in others. From this iron frame of mind he was roused by the voice of his son.

'I don't think,' said Sam, who was smoking with great composure and enjoyment, 'that if the lady wos agreeable it 'ud be wery far out o' the vay for us four to make up a club of our own like the governors does up-stairs, and let him,' Sam pointed with the stem of his pipe towards his parent, 'be the president.'

The housekeeper affably declared that it was the very thing she had been thinking of. The barber said the same. Mr. Weller said nothing, but he laid down his pipe as if in a fit of inspiration, and performed the following manoeuvres.

Unbuttoning the three lower buttons of his waistcoat and pausing for a moment to enjoy the easy flow of breath consequent upon this process, he laid violent hands upon his watch-chain, and slowly and with extreme difficulty drew from his fob an immense double-cased silver watch, which brought the lining of the pocket with it, and was not to be disentangled but by great exertions and an amazing redness of face. Having fairly got it out at last, he detached the outer case and wound it up with a key of corresponding magnitude; then put the case on again, and having applied the watch to his ear to ascertain that it was still going, gave it some half-dozen hard knocks on the table to improve its performance.

'That,' said Mr. Weller, laying it on the table with its face upwards, 'is the title and emblem o' this here society. Sammy, reach them two stools this vay for the wacant cheers. Ladies and gen'lmen, Mr. Weller's Watch is vound up and now a-goin'. Order!'

By way of enforcing this proclamation, Mr. Weller, using the watch after the manner of a president's hammer, and remarking with great pride that nothing hurt it, and that falls and concussions of all kinds materially enhanced the excellence of the works and assisted the regulator, knocked the table a great many times, and declared the association formally constituted.

'And don't let's have no grinnin' at the cheer, Samivel,' said Mr. Weller to his son, 'or I shall be committin' you to the cellar, and then p'r'aps we may get into what the 'Merrikins call a fix, and the English a qvestion o' privileges.'

Having uttered this friendly caution, the President settled himself in his chair with great dignity, and requested that Mr. Samuel would relate an anecdote.

'I've told one,' said Sam.

'Wery good, sir; tell another,' returned the chair.

'We wos a talking jist now, sir,' said Sam, turning to Slithers, 'about barbers. Pursuing that 'ere fruitful theme, sir, I'll tell you in a wery few words a romantic little story about another barber as p'r'aps you may never have heerd.'

'Samivel!' said Mr. Weller, again bringing his watch and the table into smart collision, 'address your obserwations to the cheer, sir, and not to priwate indiwiduals!'

'And if I might rise to order,' said the barber in a soft voice, and looking round him with a conciliatory smile as he leant over the table, with the knuckles of his left hand resting upon it,—'if I *might* rise to order, I would suggest that "barbers" is not exactly the kind of language which is agreeable and soothing to our feelings. You, sir, will correct me if I'm wrong, but I believe there *is* such a word in the dictionary as hairdressers.'

'Well, but suppose he wasn't a hairdresser,' suggested Sam.

'Wy then, sir, be parliamentary and call him vun all the more,' returned his father. 'In the same vay as ev'ry gen'lman in another place is a Honourable, ev'ry barber in this place is a hairdresser. Ven you read the speeches in the papers, and see as vun gen'lman says of another, "the Honourable member, if he vill allow me to call him so," you vill understand, sir, that that means, "if he vill allow me to keep up that 'ere pleasant and uniwersal fiction."'

It is a common remark, confirmed by history and experience, that great men rise with the circumstances in which they are placed. Mr. Weller came out so strong in his capacity of chairman, that Sam was for some time prevented from speaking by a grin of surprise, which held his faculties enchained, and at last subsided in a long whistle of a single note. Nay, the old gentleman appeared even to have astonished himself, and that to no small extent, as was demonstrated by the vast amount of chuckling in which he indulged, after the utterance of these lucid remarks.

'Here's the story,' said Sam. 'Vunce upon a time there wos a young hairdresser as opened a wery smart little shop vith four wax dummies in the winder, two gen'lmen and two ladies—the gen'lmen vith blue dots for their beards, wery large viskers, oudacious heads of hair, uncommon clear eyes, and nostrils of amazin' pinkness; the ladies vith their heads o' one side, their right forefingers on their lips, and their forms deweloped beautiful, in vich last respect they had the adwantage over the gen'lmen, as wasn't allowed but wery little shoulder, and terminated rayther abrupt in fancy drapery. He had also a many hair-brushes and tooth-brushes bottled up in the winder, neat glass-cases on the counter, a floor-clothed cuttin'-room up-stairs, and a weighin'- macheen in the shop, right opposite the door. But the great attraction and ornament wos the dummies, which this here young hairdresser wos constantly a runnin' out in the road to look at, and constantly a runnin' in again to touch up and polish; in short, he wos so proud on 'em, that ven Sunday come, he wos always wretched and mis'rable to think they wos behind the shutters, and looked anxiously for Monday on that account. Vun o' these dummies wos a favrite vith him beyond the others; and ven any of his acquaintance asked him wy he didn't get married—as the young ladies he know'd, in partickler, often did—he used to say, "Never! I never vill enter into the bonds of vedlock," he says, "until I meet vith a young 'ooman as realises my idea o' that 'ere fairest dummy vith the light hair. Then, and not till then," he says, "I vill approach the altar." All the young ladies he know'd as had got dark hair told him this wos wery sinful, and that he wos wurshippin' a idle; but them as wos at all near the same shade as the dummy coloured up wery much, and wos observed to think him a wery nice young man.'

'Samivel,' said Mr. Weller, gravely, 'a member o' this associashun bein' one o' that 'ere tender sex which is now immedetly referred to, I have to rekvest that you vill make no reflections.'

'I ain't a makin' any, am I?' inquired Sam.

'Order, sir!' rejoined Mr. Weller, with severe dignity. Then, sinking the chairman in the father, he added, in his usual tone of voice: 'Samivel, drive on!'

Sam interchanged a smile with the housekeeper, and proceeded:

'The young hairdresser hadn't been in the habit o' makin' this avowal above six months, ven he en-countered a young lady as wos the wery picter o' the fairest dummy. "Now," he says, "it's all up. I am a slave!" The young lady wos not only the picter o' the fairest dummy, but she was wery romantic, as the young hairdresser was, too, and he says, "O!" he says, "here's a community o' feelin', here's a flow o' soul!" he says, "here's a interchange o' sentiment!" The young lady didn't say much, o' course, but she expressed herself agreeable, and shortly artervards vent to see him vith a mutual friend. The hairdresser rushes out to meet her, but d'rectly she sees the dummies she changes colour and falls a tremblin' wiolently. "Look up, my love," says the hairdresser, "behold your imige in my winder, but not correcter than in my art!" "My imige!" she says. "Yourn!" replies the hairdresser. "But whose imige is *that*?" she says, a pinting at vun o' the gen'lmen. "No vun's, my love," he says, "it is but a idea." "A idea! " she cries: "it is a portrait, I feel it is a portrait, and that 'ere noble face must be in the millingtary!" "Wot do I hear!" says he, a crumplin' his curls. "Villiam Gibbs," she says, quite firm, "never renoo the subject. I respect you as a friend," she says, "but my affections is set upon that manly brow." "This," says the hairdresser, "is a reg'lar blight, and in it I perceive the hand of Fate. Farevell!" Vith these vords he rushes into the shop, breaks the dummy's nose vith a blow of his curlin'-irons, melts him down at the parlour fire, and never smiles artervards.'

'The young lady, Mr. Weller?' said the housekeeper.

'Why, ma'am,' said Sam, 'finding that Fate had a spite agin her, and everybody she come into contact vith, she never smiled neither, but read a deal o' poetry and pined avay,—by raythen slow degrees, for she ain't dead yet. It took a deal o' poetry to kill the hair-dresser, and some people say arter all that it was more the gin and water as caused him to be run over; p'r'aps it was a little o' both, and came o' mixing the two.'

The barber declared that Mr. Weller had related one of the most interesting stories that had ever come within his knowledge, in which opinion the housekeeper entirely concurred.

'Are you a married man, sir?' inquired Sam.

The barber replied that he had not that honour.

'I s'pose you mean to be?' said Sam.

'Well,' replied the barber, rubbing his hands smirkingly, 'I don't know, I don't think it's very likely.'

'That's a bad sign,' said Sam; 'if you'd said you meant to be vun o' these days, I should ha' looked upon you as bein' safe. You're in a wery precarious state.'

'I am not conscious of any danger, at all events,' returned the barber.

'No more wos I, sir,' said the elder Mr. Weller, interposing; 'those vere my symptoms, exactly. I've been took that vay twice. Keep your vether eye open, my friend, or you're gone.'

There was something so very solemn about this admonition, both in its matter and manner, and also in the way in which Mr. Weller still kept his eye fixed upon the unsuspecting victim, that nobody cared to speak for some little time, and might not have cared to do so for some time longer, if the housekeeper had not happened to sigh, which called off the old gentleman's attention and gave rise to a gallant inquiry whether 'there wos anythin' wery piercin' in that 'ere little heart?'

'Dear me, Mr. Weller!' said the housekeeper, laughing.

'No, but is there anythin' as agitates it?' pursued the old gentleman. 'Has it always been obderrate, always opposed to the happiness o' human creeturs? Eh? Has it?'

At this critical juncture for her blushes and confusion, the housekeeper discovered that more ale was wanted, and hastily withdrew into the cellar to draw the same, followed by the barber, who insisted on carrying the candle. Having looked after her with a very complacent expression of face, and after him with some disdain,

Mr. Weller caused his glance to travel slowly round the kitchen, until at length it rested on his son.

'Sammy,' said Mr. Weller, 'I mistrust that barber.'

'Wot for?' returned Sam; 'wot's he got to do with you? You're a nice man, you are, arter pretendin' all kinds o' terror, to go a payin' compliments and talkin' about hearts and piercers.'

The imputation of gallantry appeared to afford Mr. Weller the utmost delight, for he replied in a voice choked by suppressed laughter, and with the tears in his eyes,

'Wos I a talkin' about hearts and piercers,—wos I though, Sammy, eh?'

'Wos you? of course you wos.'

'She don't know no better, Sammy, there ain't no harm in it,—no danger, Sammy; she's only a punster. She seemed pleased, though, didn't she? O' course, she wos pleased, it's nat'ral she should be, wery nat'ral.'

'He's wain of it!' exclaimed Sam, joining in his father's mirth. 'He's actually wain!'

'Hush!' replied Mr. Weller, composing his features, 'they're a comin' back,—the little heart's a comin' back. But mark these wurds o' mine once more, and remember 'em ven your father says he said 'em. Samivel, I mistrust that 'ere deceitful barber.'

CHAPTER VI

MASTER HUMPHREY, FROM HIS CLOCK-SIDE IN THE CHIMNEY CORNER

TWO or three evenings after the institution of Mr. Weller's Watch, I thought I heard, as I walked in the garden, the voice of Mr. Weller himself at no great distance; and stopping once or twice to listen more attentively, I found that the sounds proceeded from my housekeeper's little sitting-room, which is at the back of the house. I took no further notice of the circumstance at that time, but it formed the subject of a conversation between me and my friend Jack Redburn next morning, when I found that I had not been deceived in my impression. Jack furnished me with the following particulars; and as he appeared to take extraordinary pleasure in relating them, I have begged him in future to jot down any such domestic scenes or occurrences that may please his humour, in order that they may be told in his own way. I must confess that, as Mr. Pickwick and he are constantly together, I have been influenced, in making this request, by a secret desire to know something of their proceedings.

On the evening in question, the housekeeper's room was arranged with particular care, and the housekeeper herself was very smartly dressed. The preparations, however, were not confined to mere showy demonstrations, as tea was prepared for three persons, with a small display of preserves and jams and sweet cakes, which heralded some uncommon occasion. Miss Benton (my housekeeper bears that name) was in a state of great expectation, too, frequently going to the front door and looking anxiously down the lane, and more than once observing to the servant-girl that she expected company, and hoped no accident had happened to delay them.

A modest ring at the bell at length allayed her fears, and Miss Benton, hurrying into her own room and shutting herself up, in order that she might preserve that appearance of being taken by surprise which is so essential to the polite reception of visitors, awaited their coming with a smiling countenance.

'Good ev'nin', mum,' said the older Mr. Weller, looking in at the door after a prefatory tap. 'I'm afeerd we've come in raythcr arter the time, mum, but the young colt being full o' wice, has been' a boltin' and shyin' and gettin' his leg over the traces to sich a extent that if he an't wery soon broke in, he'll wex me into a broken heart, and then he'll never be brought out no more except to learn his letters from the writin' on his grandfather's tombstone.'

With these pathetic words, which were addressed to something outside the door about two feet six from the ground, Mr. Weller introduced a very small boy firmly set upon a couple of very sturdy legs, who looked as if nothing could ever knock him down. Besides having a very round face strongly resembling Mr. Weller's, and a stout little body of exactly his build, this young gentleman, standing with his little legs very wide apart, as if the top-boots were familiar to them, actually winked upon the housekeeper with his infant eye, in imitation of his grandfather.

'There's a naughty boy, mum,' said Mr. Weller, bursting with delight, 'there's a immoral Tony. Wos there ever a little chap o' four year and eight months old as vinked his eye at a strange lady afore?'

As little affected by this observation as by the former appeal to his feelings, Master Weller elevated in the air a small model of a coach whip which he carried in his hand, and addressing the housekeeper with a shrill 'ya—hip!' inquired if she was 'going down the road;' at which happy adaptation of a lesson he had been taught from infancy, Mr. Weller could restrain his feelings no longer, but gave him twopence on the spot.

'It's in wain to deny it, mum,' said Mr. Weller, 'this here is a boy arter his grandfather's own heart, and beats out all the boys as ever wos or will be. Though at the same time, mum,' added Mr. Weller, trying to look gravely down upon his favourite, 'it was wery wrong on him to want to—over all the posts as we come along, and wery cruel on him to force poor grandfather to lift him cross- legged over every vun of 'em. He wouldn't pass vun single blessed post, mum, and at the top o' the lane there's seven-and-forty on 'em all in a row, and wery close together.'

Here Mr. Weller, whose feelings were in a perpetual conflict between pride in his grandson's achievements and a sense of his own responsibility, and the importance of impressing him with moral truths, burst into a fit of laughter, and suddenly checking himself, remarked in a severe tone that little boys as made their grandfathers put 'em over posts never went to heaven at any price.

By this time the housekeeper had made tea, and little Tony, placed on a chair beside her, with his eyes nearly on a level with the top of the table, was provided with various delicacies which yielded him extreme contentment. The housekeeper (who seemed rather afraid of the child, notwithstanding her caresses) then patted him on the head, and declared that he was the finest boy she had ever seen.

'Wy, mum,' said Mr. Weller, 'I don't think you'll see a many sich, and that's the truth. But if my son Samivel vould give me my vay, mum, and only dis-pense vith his—*might* I wenter to say the vurd?'

'What word, Mr. Weller?' said the housekeeper, blushing slightly.

'Petticuts, mum,' returned that gentleman, laying his hand upon the garments of his grandson. 'If my son Samivel, mum, vould only dis-pense vith these here, you'd see such a alteration in his appearance, as the imagination can't depicter.'

'But what would you have the child wear instead, Mr. Weller?' said the housekeeper.

'I've offered my son Samivel, mum, agen and agen,' returned the old gentleman, 'to purwide him at my own cost vith a suit o' clothes as 'ud be the makin' on him, and form his mind in infancy for those pursuits as I hope the family o' the Vellers vill alvays dewote themselves to. Tony, my boy, tell the lady wot them clothes are, as grandfather says, father ought to let you vear.'

'A little white hat and a little sprig weskut and little knee cords and little top-boots and a little green coat with little bright buttons and a little welwet collar,' replied Tony, with great readiness and no stops.

'That's the cos-toom, mum,' said Mr. Weller, looking proudly at the housekeeper. 'Once make sich a model on him as that, and you'd say he WOS an angel!'

Perhaps the housekeeper thought that in such a guise young Tony would look more like the angel at Islington than anything else of that name, or perhaps she was disconcerted to find her previously- conceived ideas disturbed, as angels are not commonly represented in top-boots and sprig waistcoats. She coughed doubtfully, but said nothing.

'How many brothers and sisters have you, my dear?' she asked, after a short silence.

'One brother and no sister at all,' replied Tony. 'Sam his name is, and so's my father's. Do you know my father?'

'O yes, I know him,' said the housekeeper, graciously.

'Is my father fond of you?' pursued Tony.

'I hope so,' rejoined the smiling housekeeper.

Tony considered a moment, and then said, 'Is my grandfather fond of you?'

This would seem a very easy question to answer, but instead of replying to it, the housekeeper smiled in great confusion, and said that really children did ask such extraordinary questions that it was the most difficult thing in the world to talk to them. Mr. Weller took upon himself to reply that he was very fond of the lady; but the housekeeper entreating that he would not put such things into the child's head, Mr. Weller shook his own while she looked another way, and seemed to be troubled with a misgiving that captivation was in progress. It was, perhaps, on this account that he changed the subject precipitately.

'It's wery wrong in little boys to make game o' their grandfathers, an't it, mum?' said Mr. Weller, shaking his head waggishly, until Tony looked at him, when he counterfeited the deepest dejection and sorrow.

'O, very sad!' assented the housekeeper. 'But I hope no little boys do that?'

'There is vun young Turk, mum,' said Mr. Weller, 'as havin' seen his grandfather a little overcome vith drink on the occasion of a friend's birthday, goes a reelin' and staggerin' about the house, and makin' believe that he's the old gen'lm'n.'

'O, quite shocking!' cried the housekeeper,

'Yes, mum,' said Mr. Weller; 'and previously to so doin', this here young traitor that I'm a speakin' of, pinches his little nose to make it red, and then he gives a hiccup and says, "I'm all right," he says; "give us another song!" Ha, ha! "Give us another song," he says. Ha, ha, ha!'

In his excessive delight, Mr. Weller was quite unmindful of his moral responsibility, until little Tony kicked up his legs, and laughing immoderately, cried, 'That was me, that was;' whereupon the grandfather, by a great effort, became extremely solemn.

'No, Tony, not you,' said Mr. Weller. 'I hope it warn't you, Tony. It must ha' been that 'ere naughty little chap as comes sometimes out o' the empty watch-box round the corner,—that same little chap as wos found standing on the table afore the looking-glass, pretending to shave himself vith a oyster-knife.'

'He didn't hurt himself, I hope?' observed the housekeeper.

'Not he, mum,' said Mr. Weller proudly; 'bless your heart, you might trust that 'ere boy vith a steam-engine a'most, he's such a knowin' young'—but suddenly recollecting himself and observing that Tony perfectly understood and appreciated the compliment, the old gentleman groaned and observed that 'it wos all wery shockin'—wery.'

'O, he's a bad 'un,' said Mr. Weller, 'is that 'ere watch-box boy, makin' such a noise and litter in the back yard, he does, waterin' wooden horses and feedin' of 'em vith grass, and perpetivally spillin' his little brother out of a veelbarrow and frightenin' his mother out of her vits, at the wery moment wen she's expectin' to increase his stock of happiness vith another play-feller,—O, he's a bad one! He's even gone so far as to put on a pair of paper spectacles as he got his father to make for him, and walk up and down the garden vith his hands behind him in imitation of Mr. Pickwick,—but Tony don't do sich things, O no!'

'O no!' echoed Tony.

'He knows better, he does,' said Mr. Weller. 'He knows that if he wos to come sich games as these nobody wouldn't love him, and that his grandfather in partickler couldn't abear the sight on him; for vich reasons Tony's always good.'

'Always good,' echoed Tony; and his grandfather immediately took him on his knee and kissed him, at the same time, with many nods and winks, slyly pointing at the child's head with his thumb, in order that the housekeeper, otherwise deceived by the admirable manner in which he (Mr. Weller) had sustained his character, might not suppose that any other young gentleman was referred to, and might clearly understand that the boy of the watch-box was but an imaginary creation, and a fetch of Tony himself, invented for his improvement and reformation.

Not confining himself to a mere verbal description of his grandson's abilities, Mr. Weller, when tea was finished, invited him by various gifts of pence and halfpence to smoke imaginary pipes, drink visionary beer from real pots, imitate his grandfather without reserve, and in particular to go through the drunken scene, which threw the old gentleman into ecstasies and filled the housekeeper with wonder. Nor was Mr. Weller's pride satisfied with even this display, for when he took his leave he carried the child, like some rare and astonishing curiosity, first to the barber's house and afterwards to the tobacconist's, at each of which places he repeated his performances with the utmost effect to applauding and delighted audiences. It was half-past nine o'clock when Mr. Weller was last seen carrying him home upon his shoulder, and it has been whispered abroad that at that time the infant Tony was rather intoxicated.

I was musing the other evening upon the characters and incidents with which I had been so long engaged; wondering how I could ever have looked forward with pleasure to the completion of my tale, and reproaching myself for having done so, as if it were a kind of cruelty to those companions of my solitude whom I had now dismissed, and could never again recall; when my clock struck ten. Punctual to the hour, my friends appeared.

On our last night of meeting, we had finished the story which the reader has just concluded. Our conversation took the same current as the meditations which the entrance of my friends had interrupted, and The Old Curiosity Shop was the staple of our discourse.

I may confide to the reader now, that in connection with this little history I had something upon my mind; something to communicate which I had all along with difficulty repressed; something I had deemed it, during the progress of the story, necessary to its interest to disguise, and which, now that it was over, I wished, and was yet reluctant, to disclose.

To conceal anything from those to whom I am attached, is not in my nature. I can never close my lips where I have opened my heart. This temper, and the consciousness of having done some violence to it in my narrative, laid me under a restraint which I should have had great difficulty in overcoming, but for a timely remark from Mr. Miles, who, as I hinted in a former paper, is a gentleman of business habits, and of great exactness and propriety in all his transactions.

'I could have wished,' my friend objected, 'that we had been made acquainted with the single gentleman's name. I don't like his withholding his name. It made me look upon him at first with suspicion, and caused me to doubt his moral character, I assure you. I am fully satisfied by this time of his being a worthy creature; but in this respect he certainly would not appear to have acted at all like a man of business.'

'My friends,' said I, drawing to the table, at which they were by this time seated in their usual chairs, 'do you remember that this story bore another title besides that one we have so often heard of late?'

Mr. Miles had his pocket-book out in an instant, and referring to an entry therein, rejoined, 'Certainly. Personal Adventures of Master Humphrey. Here it is. I made a note of it at the time.'

I was about to resume what I had to tell them, when the same Mr. Miles again interrupted me, observing that the narrative originated in a personal adventure of my own, and that was no doubt the reason for its being thus designated.

This led me to the point at once.

'You will one and all forgive me,' I returned, 'if for the greater convenience of the story, and for its better introduction, that adventure was fictitious. I had my share, indeed,—no light or trivial one,—in the pages we have read, but it was not the share I feigned to have at first. The younger brother, the single gentleman, the nameless actor in this little drama, stands before you now.'

It was easy to see they had not expected this disclosure.

'Yes,' I pursued. 'I can look back upon my part in it with a calm, half-smiling pity for myself as for some other man. But I am he, indeed; and now the chief sorrows of my life are yours.'

I need not say what true gratification I derived from the sympathy and kindness with which this acknowledgment was received; nor how often it had risen to my lips before; nor how difficult I had found it—how impossible, when I came to those passages which touched me most, and most nearly concerned me—to sustain the character I had assumed. It is enough to say that I replaced in the clock-case the record of so many trials,—sorrowfully, it is true, but with a softened sorrow which was almost pleasure; and felt that in living through the past again, and communicating to others the lesson it had helped to teach me, I had been a happier man.

We lingered so long over the leaves from which I had read, that as I consigned them to their former resting-place, the hand of my trusty clock pointed to twelve, and there came towards us upon the wind the voice of the deep and distant bell of St. Paul's as it struck the hour of midnight.

'This,' said I, returning with a manuscript I had taken at the moment, from the same repository, 'to be opened to such music, should be a tale where London's face by night is darkly seen, and where some deed of such a time as this is dimly shadowed out. Which of us here has seen the working of that great machine whose voice has just now ceased?'

Mr. Pickwick had, of course, and so had Mr. Miles. Jack and my deaf friend were in the minority.

I had seen it but a few days before, and could not help telling them of the fancy I had about it.

I paid my fee of twopence upon entering, to one of the money- changers who sit within the Temple; and falling, after a few turns up and down, into the quiet train of thought which such a place awakens, paced the echoing stones like some old monk whose present world lay all within its walls. As I looked afar up into the lofty dome, I could not help wondering what were his reflections whose genius reared that mighty pile, when, the last small wedge of timber fixed, the last nail driven into its home for many centuries, the clang of hammers, and the hum of busy voices gone, and the Great Silence whole years of noise had helped to make, reigning undisturbed around, he mused, as I did now, upon his work, and lost himself amid its vast extent. I could not quite determine whether the contemplation of it would impress him with a sense of greatness or of insignificance; but when I remembered how long a time it had taken to erect, in how short a space it might be traversed even to its remotest parts, for how brief a term he, or any of those who cared to bear his name, would live to see it, or know of its existence, I imagined him far more melancholy than proud, and looking with regret upon his labour done. With these thoughts in my mind, I began to ascend, almost unconsciously, the flight of steps leading to the several wonders of the building, and found myself before a barrier where another money-taker sat, who demanded which among them I would choose to see. There were the stone gallery, he said, and the whispering gallery, the geometrical staircase, the room of models, the clock—the clock being quite in my way, I stopped him there, and chose that sight from all the rest.

I groped my way into the Turret which it occupies, and saw before me, in a kind of loft, what seemed to be a great, old oaken press with folding doors. These being thrown back by the attendant (who was sleeping when I came upon him, and looked a drowsy fellow, as though his close companionship with Time had made him quite indifferent to it), disclosed a complicated crowd of wheels and chains in iron and brass,—great, sturdy, rattling engines,—suggestive of breaking a finger put in here or there, and grinding the bone to powder,—and these were the Clock! Its very pulse, if I may use the word, was like no other clock. It did not mark the flight of every moment with a gentle second stroke, as though it would check old Time, and have him stay his pace in pity, but measured it with one sledge-hammer beat, as if its business were to crush the seconds as they came trooping on, and remorselessly to clear a path before the Day of Judgment.

I sat down opposite to it, and hearing its regular and never- changing voice, that one deep constant note, uppermost amongst all the noise and clatter in the streets below,—marking that, let that tumult rise or fall, go on or stop,—let it be night or noon, to-morrow or to-day, this year or next,—it still performed its functions with the same dull constancy, and regulated the progress of the life around, the fancy came upon me that this was London's Heart,—and that when it should cease to beat, the City would be no more.

It is night. Calm and unmoved amidst the scenes that darkness favours, the great heart of London throbs in its Giant breast. Wealth and beggary, vice and virtue, guilt and innocence, repletion and the direst hunger, all treading on each other and crowding together, are gathered round it. Draw but a little circle above the clustering housetops, and you shall have within its space everything, with its opposite extreme and contradiction, close beside. Where yonder feeble light is shining, a man is but this moment dead. The taper at a few yards' distance is seen by eyes that have this instant opened on the world. There are two houses separated by but an inch or two of wall. In one, there are quiet minds at rest; in the other, a waking conscience that one might think would trouble the very air. In that close corner where the roofs shrink down and cower together as if to hide their secrets from the handsome street hard by, there are such dark crimes, such miseries and horrors, as could be hardly told in whispers. In the handsome street, there are folks asleep who have dwelt there all their lives, and have no more knowledge of these things than if they had never been, or were transacted at the remotest limits of the world,—who, if they were hinted at, would shake their heads, look wise, and frown, and say they were impossible, and out of Nature,—as if all great towns were not. Does not this Heart of London, that nothing moves, nor stops, nor quickens,—that goes on the same let what will be done, does it not express the City's character well?

The day begins to break, and soon there is the hum and noise of life. Those who have spent the night on doorsteps and cold stones crawl off to beg; they who have slept in beds come forth to their occupation, too, and business is astir. The fog of sleep rolls slowly off, and London shines awake. The streets are filled with carriages and people gaily clad. The jails are full, too, to the throat, nor have the workhouses or hospitals much room to spare. The courts of law are crowded. Taverns have their regular frequenters by this time, and every mart of traffic has its throng. Each of these places is a world, and has its own inhabitants; each is distinct from, and almost unconscious of the existence of any other. There are some few people well to do, who remember to have heard it said, that numbers of men and women—thousands, they think it was—get up in London every day, unknowing where to lay their heads at night; and that there are quarters of the town where misery and famine always are. They don't believe it quite,—there may be some truth in it, but it is exaggerated, of course. So, each of these thousand worlds goes on, intent upon itself, until night comes again,—first with its lights and pleasures, and its cheerful streets; then with its guilt and darkness.

Heart of London, there is a moral in thy every stroke! as I look on at thy indomitable working, which neither death, nor press of life, nor grief, nor gladness out of doors will influence one jot, I seem to hear a voice within thee which sinks into my heart, bidding me, as I elbow my way among the crowd, have some thought for the meanest wretch that passes, and, being a man, to turn away with scorn and pride from none that bear the human shape.

I am by no means sure that I might not have been tempted to enlarge upon the subject, had not the papers that lay before me on the table been a silent reproach for even this digression. I took them up again when I had got thus far, and seriously prepared to read.

The handwriting was strange to me, for the manuscript had been fairly copied. As it is against our rules, in such a case, to inquire into the authorship until the reading is concluded, I could only glance at the different faces round me, in search of some expression which should betray the writer. Whoever he might be, he was prepared for this, and gave no sign for my enlightenment.

I had the papers in my hand, when my deaf friend interposed with a suggestion.

'It has occurred to me,' he said, 'bearing in mind your sequel to the tale we have finished, that if such of us as have anything to relate of our own lives could interweave it with our contribution to the Clock, it would be well to do so. This need be no restraint upon us, either as to time, or place, or incident, since any real passage of this kind may be surrounded by fictitious circumstances, and represented by fictitious characters. What if we make this an article of agreement among ourselves?'

The proposition was cordially received, but the difficulty appeared to be that here was a long story written before we had thought of it.

'Unless,' said I, 'it should have happened that the writer of this tale—which is not impossible, for men are apt to do so when they write—has actually mingled with it something of his own endurance and experience.'

Nobody spoke, but I thought I detected in one quarter that this was really the case.

'If I have no assurance to the contrary,' I added, therefore, 'I shall take it for granted that he has done so, and that even these papers come within our new agreement. Everybody being mute, we hold that understanding if you please.'

And here I was about to begin again, when Jack informed us softly, that during the progress of our last narrative, Mr. Weller's Watch had adjourned its sittings from the kitchen, and regularly met outside our door, where he had no doubt that august body would be found at the present moment. As this was for the convenience of listening to our stories, he submitted that they might be suffered to come in, and hear them more pleasantly.

To this we one and all yielded a ready assent, and the party being discovered, as Jack had supposed, and invited to walk in, entered (though not without great confusion at having been detected), and were accommodated with chairs at a little distance.

Then, the lamp being trimmed, the fire well stirred and burning brightly, the hearth clean swept, the curtains closely drawn, the clock wound up, we entered on our new story.

It is again midnight. My fire burns cheerfully; the room is filled with my old friend's sober voice; and I am left to muse upon the story we have just now finished.

It makes me smile, at such a time as this, to think if there were any one to see me sitting in my easy-chair, my gray head hanging down, my eyes bent thoughtfully upon the glowing embers, and my crutch—emblem of my helplessness—lying upon the hearth at my feet, how solitary I should seem. Yet though I am the sole tenant of this chimney-corner, though I am childless and old, I have no sense of loneliness at this hour; but am the centre of a silent group whose company I love.

Thus, even age and weakness have their consolations. If I were a younger man, if I were more active, more strongly bound and tied to life, these visionary friends would shun me, or I should desire to fly from them. Being what I am, I can court their society, and delight in it; and pass whole hours in picturing to myself the shadows that perchance flock every night into this chamber, and in imagining with pleasure what kind of interest they have in the frail, feeble mortal who is its sole inhabitant.

All the friends I have ever lost I find again among these visitors. I love to fancy their spirits hovering about me, feeling still some earthly kindness for their old companion, and watching his decay. 'He is weaker, he declines apace, he draws nearer and nearer to us, and will soon be conscious of our existence.' What is there to alarm me in this? It is encouragement and hope.

These thoughts have never crowded on me half so fast as they have done to-night. Faces I had long forgotten have become familiar to me once again; traits I had endeavoured to recall for years have come before me in an instant; nothing is changed but me; and even I can be my former self at will.

Raising my eyes but now to the face of my old clock, I remember, quite involuntarily, the veneration, not unmixed with a sort of childish awe, with which I used to sit and watch it as it ticked, unheeded in a dark staircase corner. I recollect looking more grave and steady when I met its dusty face, as if, having that strange kind of life within it, and being free from all excess of vulgar appetite, and warning all the house by night and day, it were a sage. How often have I listened to it as it told the beads of time, and wondered at its constancy! How often watched it slowly pointing round the dial, and, while I panted for the eagerly expected hour to come, admired, despite myself, its steadiness of purpose and lofty freedom from all human strife, impatience, and desire!

I thought it cruel once. It was very hard of heart, to my mind, I remember. It was an old servant even then; and I felt as though it ought to show some sorrow; as though it wanted sympathy with us in our distress, and were a dull, heartless, mercenary creature. Ah! how soon I learnt to know that in its ceaseless going on, and in its being checked or stayed by nothing, lay its greatest kindness, and the only balm for grief and wounded peace of mind.

To-night, to-night, when this tranquillity and calm are on my spirits, and memory presents so many shifting scenes before me, I take my quiet stand at will by many a fire that has been long extinguished, and mingle with the cheerful group that cluster round it. If I could be sorrowful in such a mood, I should grow sad to think what a poor blot I was upon their youth and beauty once, and now how few remain to put me to the blush; I should grow sad to think that such among them as I sometimes meet with in my daily walks are scarcely less infirm than I; that time has brought us to a level; and that all distinctions fade and vanish as we take our trembling steps towards the grave.

But memory was given us for better purposes than this, and mine is not a torment, but a source of pleasure. To muse upon the gaiety and youth I have known suggests to me glad scenes of harmless mirth that may be passing now. From contemplating them apart, I soon become an actor in these little dramas, and humouring my fancy, lose myself among the beings it invokes.

When my fire is bright and high, and a warm blush mantles in the walls and ceiling of this ancient room; when my clock makes cheerful music, like one of those chirping insects who delight in the warm hearth, and are sometimes, by a good superstition, looked upon as the harbingers of fortune and plenty to that household in whose mercies they put their humble trust; when everything is in a ruddy genial glow, and there are voices in the crackling flame, and smiles in its flashing light, other smiles and other voices congregate around me, invading, with their pleasant harmony, the silence of the time.

For then a knot of youthful creatures gather round my fireside, and the room re-echoes to their merry voices. My solitary chair no longer holds its ample place before the fire, but is wheeled into a smaller corner, to leave more room for the broad circle formed about the cheerful hearth. I have sons, and daughters, and grandchildren, and we are assembled on some occasion of rejoicing common to us all. It is a birthday, perhaps, or perhaps it may be Christmas time; but be it what it may, there is rare holiday among us; we are full of glee.

In the chimney-comer, opposite myself, sits one who has grown old beside me. She is changed, of course; much changed; and yet I recognise the girl even in that gray hair and wrinkled brow. Glancing from the laughing child who half hides in her ample skirts, and half peeps out,—and from her to the little matron of twelve years old, who sits so womanly and so demure at no great distance from me,—and from her again, to a fair girl in the full bloom of early womanhood, the centre of the group, who has glanced more than once towards the opening door, and by whom the children, whispering and tittering among themselves, *will* leave a vacant chair, although she bids them not,—I see her image thrice repeated, and feel how long it is before one form and set of features wholly pass away, if ever, from among the living. While I am dwelling upon this, and tracing out the gradual change from infancy to youth, from youth to perfect growth, from that to age, and thinking, with an old man's pride, that she is comely yet, I feel a slight thin hand upon my arm, and, looking down, see seated at my feet a crippled boy,—a gentle, patient child,—whose aspect I know well. He rests upon a little crutch,—I know it too,—and leaning on it as he climbs my footstool, whispers in my ear, 'I am hardly one of these, dear grandfather, although I love them dearly. They are very kind to me, but you will be kinder still, I know.'

I have my hand upon his neck, and stoop to kiss him, when my clock strikes, my chair is in its old spot, and I am alone.

What if I be? What if this fireside be tenantless, save for the presence of one weak old man? From my house-top I can look upon a hundred homes, in every one of which these social companions are matters of reality. In my daily walks I pass a thousand men whose cares are all forgotten, whose labours are made light, whose dull routine of work from day to day is cheered and brightened by their glimpses of domestic joy at home. Amid the struggles of this struggling town what cheerful sacrifices are made; what toil endured with readiness; what patience shown and fortitude displayed for the mere sake of home and its affections! Let me thank Heaven that I can people my fireside with shadows such as these; with shadows of bright objects that exist in crowds about me; and let me say, 'I am alone no more.'

I never was less so—I write it with a grateful heart—than I am to night. Recollections of the past and visions of the present come to bear me company; the meanest man to whom I have ever given alms appears, to add his mite of peace and comfort to my stock; and whenever the fire within me shall grow cold, to light my path upon this earth no more, I pray that it may be at such an hour as this, and when I love the world as well as I do now.

THE DEAF GENTLEMAN FROM HIS OWN APARTMENT

Our dear friend laid down his pen at the end of the foregoing paragraph, to take it up no more. I little thought ever to employ mine upon so sorrowful a task as that which he has left me, and to which I now devote it.

As he did not appear among us at his usual hour next morning, we knocked gently at his door. No answer being given, it was softly opened; and then, to our surprise, we saw him seated before the ashes of his fire, with a little table I was accustomed to set at his elbow when I left him for the night at a short distance from him, as though he had pushed it away with the idea of rising and retiring to his bed. His crutch and footstool lay at his feet as usual, and he was dressed in his chamber-gown, which he had put on before I left him. He was reclining in his chair, in his accustomed posture, with his face towards the fire, and seemed absorbed in meditation,—indeed, at first, we almost hoped he was.

Going up to him, we found him dead. I have often, very often, seen him sleeping, and always peacefully, but I never saw him look so calm and tranquil. His face wore a serene, benign expression, which had impressed me very strongly when we last shook hands; not that he had ever had any other look, God knows; but there was something in this so very spiritual, so strangely and indefinably allied to youth, although his head was gray and venerable, that it was new even in him. It came upon me all at once when on some slight pretence he called me back upon the previous night to take me by the hand again, and once more say, 'God bless you.'

A bell-rope hung within his reach, but he had not moved towards it; nor had he stirred, we all agreed, except, as I have said, to push away his table, which he could have done, and no doubt did, with a very slight motion of his hand. He had relapsed for a moment into his late train of meditation, and, with a thoughtful smile upon his face, had died.

I had long known it to be his wish that whenever this event should come to pass we might be all assembled in the house. I therefore lost no time in sending for Mr. Pickwick and for Mr. Miles, both of whom arrived before the messenger's return.

It is not my purpose to dilate upon the sorrow and affectionate emotions of which I was at once the witness and the sharer. But I may say, of the humbler mourners, that his faithful housekeeper was fairly heart-broken; that the poor barber would not be comforted; and that I shall respect the homely truth and warmth of heart of Mr. Weller and his son to the last moment of my life.

'And the sweet old creetur, sir,' said the elder Mr. Weller to me in the afternoon, 'has bolted. Him as had no wice, and was so free from temper that a infant might ha' drove him, has been took at last with that 'ere unawoidable fit o' staggers as we all must come to, and gone off his feed for ever! I see him,' said the old gentleman, with a moisture in his eye, which could not be mistaken,—'I see him gettin', every journey, more and more groggy; I says to Samivel, "My boy! the Grey's a-goin' at the knees;" and now my predilictions is fatally werified, and him as I could never do enough to serve or show my likin' for, is up the great uniwersal spout o' natur'.'

I was not the less sensible of the old man's attachment because he expressed it in his peculiar manner. Indeed, I can truly assert of both him and his son, that notwithstanding the extraordinary dialogues they held together, and the strange commentaries and corrections with which each of them illustrated the other's speech, I do not think it possible to exceed the sincerity of their regret; and that I am sure their thoughtfulness and anxiety in anticipating the discharge of many little offices of sympathy would have done honour to the most delicate-minded persons.

Our friend had frequently told us that his will would be found in a box in the Clock-case, the key of which was in his writing-desk. As he had told us also that he desired it to be opened immediately after his death, whenever that should happen, we met together that night for the fulfilment of his request.

We found it where he had told us, wrapped in a sealed paper, and with it a codicil of recent date, in which he named Mr. Miles and Mr. Pickwick his executors,—as having no need of any greater benefit from his estate than a generous token (which he bequeathed to them) of his friendship and remembrance.

After pointing out the spot in which he wished his ashes to repose, he gave to 'his dear old friends,' Jack Redburn and myself, his house, his books, his furniture,—in short, all that his house contained; and with this legacy more ample means of maintaining it in its present state than we, with our habits and at our terms of life, can ever exhaust. Besides these gifts, he left to us, in trust, an annual sum of no insignificant amount, to be distributed in charity among his accustomed pensioners—they are a long list—and such other claimants on his bounty as might, from time to time, present themselves. And as true charity not only covers a multitude of sins, but includes a multitude of virtues, such as forgiveness, liberal construction, gentleness and mercy to the faults of others, and the remembrance of our own imperfections and advantages, he bade us not inquire too closely into the venial errors of the poor, but finding that they *were* poor, first to relieve and then endeavour—at an advantage—to reclaim them.

To the housekeeper he left an annuity, sufficient for her comfortable maintenance and support through life. For the barber, who had attended him many years, he made a similar provision. And I may make two remarks in this place: first, that I think this pair are very likely to club their means together and make a match of it; and secondly, that I think my friend had this result in his mind, for I have heard him say, more than once, that he could not concur with the generality of mankind in censuring equal marriages made in later life, since there were many cases in which such unions could not fail to be a wise and rational source of happiness to both parties.

The elder Mr. Weller is so far from viewing this prospect with any feelings of jealousy, that he appears to be very much relieved by its contemplation; and his son, if I am not mistaken, participates in this feeling. We are all of opinion, however, that the old gentleman's danger, even at its crisis, was very slight, and that he merely laboured under one of those transitory weaknesses to which persons of his temperament are now and then liable, and which become less and less alarming at every return, until they wholly subside. I have no doubt he will remain a jolly old widower for the rest of his life, as he has already inquired of me, with much gravity, whether a writ of habeas corpus would enable him to settle his property upon Tony beyond the possibility of recall; and has, in my presence, conjured his son, with tears in his eyes, that in the event of his ever becoming amorous again, he will put him in a strait-waistcoat until the fit is past, and distinctly inform the lady that his property is 'made over.'

Although I have very little doubt that Sam would dutifully comply with these injunctions in a case of extreme necessity, and that he would do so with perfect composure and coolness, I do not apprehend things will ever come to that pass, as the old gentleman seems perfectly happy in the society of his son, his pretty daughter-in- law, and his grandchildren, and has solemnly announced his determination to 'take arter the old 'un in all respects;' from which I infer that it is his intention to regulate his conduct by the model of Mr. Pickwick, who will certainly set him the example of a single life.

I have diverged for a moment from the subject with which I set out, for I know that my friend was interested in these little matters, and I have a natural tendency to linger upon any topic that occupied his thoughts or gave him pleasure and amusement. His remaining wishes are very briefly told. He desired that we would make him the frequent subject of our conversation; at the same time, that we would never speak of him with an air of gloom or restraint, but frankly, and as one whom we still loved and hoped to meet again. He trusted that the old house would wear no aspect of mourning, but that it would be lively and cheerful; and that we would not remove or cover up his picture, which hangs in our dining-room, but make it our companion as he had been. His own room, our place of meeting, remains, at his desire, in its accustomed state; our seats are placed about the table as of old; his easy-chair, his desk, his crutch, his footstool, hold their accustomed places, and the clock stands in its familiar corner. We go into the chamber at stated times to see that all is as it should be, and to take care that the light and air are not shut out, for on that point he expressed a strong solicitude. But it was his fancy that the apartment should not be inhabited; that it should be religiously preserved in this condition, and that the voice of his old companion should be heard no more.

My own history may be summed up in very few words; and even those I should have spared the reader but for my friend's allusion to me some time since. I have no deeper sorrow than the loss of a child,—an only daughter, who is living, and who fled from her father's house but a few weeks before our friend and I first met. I had never spoken of this even to him, because I have always loved her, and I could not bear to tell him of her error until I could tell him also of her sorrow and regret. Happily I was enabled to do so some time ago. And it will not be long, with Heaven's leave, before she is restored to me; before I find in her and her husband the support of my declining years.

For my pipe, it is an old relic of home, a thing of no great worth, a poor trifle, but sacred to me for her sake.

Thus, since the death of our venerable friend, Jack Redburn and I have been the sole tenants of the old house; and, day by day, have lounged together in his favourite walks. Mindful of his injunctions, we have long been able to speak of him with ease and cheerfulness, and to remember him as he would be remembered. From certain allusions which Jack has dropped, to his having been deserted and cast off in early life, I am inclined to believe that some passages of his youth may possibly be shadowed out in the history of Mr. Chester and his son, but seeing that he avoids the subject, I have not pursued it.

My task is done. The chamber in which we have whiled away so many hours, not, I hope, without some pleasure and some profit, is deserted; our happy hour of meeting strikes no more; the chimney-corner has grown cold; and MASTER HUMPHREY'S CLOCK has stopped for ever.